BETSY'S WINTERHOUSE

By the Same Author

EDDIE THE DOG HOLDER. 1966
ROBERT ROWS THE RIVER. 1965
EDDIE'S GREEN THUMB. 1964
HERE COMES THE BUS! 1963
SNOWBOUND WITH BETSY. 1962
ANNIE PAT AND EDDIE. 1960
EDDIE AND LOUELLA. 1959
BETSY'S WINTERHOUSE. 1958
EDDIE MAKES MUSIC. 1957
BETSY'S BUSY SUMMER. 1956
EDDIE AND HIS BIG DEALS. 1955
BETSY AND THE CIRCUS. 1954
EDDIE'S PAY DIRT. 1953
THE MIXED-UP TWINS. 1952
EDDIE AND GARDENIA. 1951
BETSY'S LITTLE STAR. 1950
EDDIE AND THE FIRE ENGINE. 1949
PENNY GOES TO CAMP. 1948
LITTLE EDDIE. 1947
Published by William Morrow & Company

PENNY AND PETER. 1946
BETSY AND THE BOYS. 1945
HERE'S A PENNY. 1944
BACK TO SCHOOL WITH BETSY. 1943
PRIMROSE DAY. 1942
BETSY AND BILLY. 1941
TWO AND TWO ARE FOUR. 1940
"B" IS FOR BETSY. 1939
Published by Harcourt, Brace & World

BETSY'S
WINTERHOUSE

Written and Illustrated by
CAROLYN HAYWOOD

WILLIAM MORROW AND COMPANY
New York, 1958

To the Lillys:
Charlie, Dorothy, Christie, and Debbie

CONTENTS

1 Betsy's Winterhouse 13

2 Christmas Carols and the Birthday Tree 33

3 The New Year Cakes 53

4 Linda's Dream Cat 73

5 A Name for a Lady Cat 89

6 How Soapie Was Done in Soap 109

7 Lost-and-Found Cats 128

8 April Fool for Whom? 148

9 May Baskets 169

BETSY'S WINTERHOUSE

CHAPTER 1

BETSY'S WINTERHOUSE

IT WAS November and the maple trees in front of Betsy's house were bleak and bare. When the cold wind blew through the oak trees near Betsy's summer-house, their brown leaves rattled like wrapping paper.

Betsy looked at the summerhouse, all boarded up for the winter. She thought of the fun that she and her little sister Star and all their friends had had in the long summer days. The summerhouse had been a place of their own, where there were no things that belonged to grownups, no things to upset, no things to get lost. No one ever came there and said, "I left an important paper here. What did you do with it?" or, "Be careful of my beautiful china shepherdess!"

Betsy began to wish that there was a place in the winter, like the summerhouse in the summer, where she and Star and their friends could play. A place of their very own.

That evening at dinner, Betsy said, "I wish we could have a winterhouse."

"Whatever do you mean, Betsy?" said her mother. "What is a winterhouse?"

"Well, we have a summerhouse to play in in the summer," said Betsy, "so there should be a winterhouse to play in in the winter."

"And where do you think would be a good place to build this winterhouse?" asked her father. "Right in the center of the living room, I suppose."

Betsy laughed. "Oh, no!" she said. "The living room is Mother's and your winterhouse. You let Star and me play in it, but it isn't ours."

"Betsy!" said her father. "You're taking my appetite away with this sad story. You should have an Eskimo father. Then he could build you a winterhouse of snow and ice. Very cozy!"

Betsy laughed again. She knew that Father was teasing her. "Anyway, it's true," she said. "Star and I need a winterhouse."

"Yes!" said Star. "We need a winterhouse." She had no idea what a winterhouse could be, but she liked the summerhouse and she always agreed with Betsy in such matters.

Nothing more was said about the winterhouse, but on Saturday morning Betsy found her father working at his desk with a pencil and a ruler and a large sheet of paper. Every once in a while he ran down to the basement with a yardstick in his hand.

"What are you doing, Father?" Betsy asked.

15

"I'm getting ready to build your winterhouse," said Father.

"Oh, Father!" cried Betsy. "Are you really? Where are you going to build it?"

"In the basement," her father replied. "Most people would call what I'm building a rumpus room, but if we stick to your name, winterhouse, perhaps it won't be as noisy."

"Oh, Father!" said Betsy. "How wonderful! How long will it take you to build it?"

"I'll do it just as quickly as possible," her father replied.

Betsy rushed off to tell Star the good news.

Now Betsy's father was as busy as the Seven Little Dwarfs. He worked in the basement in the evenings, and he worked on Saturdays too. He sawed and he hammered. Lumber and wallboard lay piled on the basement floor. He put up a partition to separate the new room from the part of the basement where the washing machine and laundry tubs were. Then he put

16

up a door. When the walls of the room were finished, he fastened slabs of material on the ceiling that Betsy said looked like dominoes and Star said looked like waffles. Father said that they would make the room quieter. He laid tile with bright-colored spots on the floor, and he said, "Now if you drop paint on this floor, it will be just one more spot."

Betsy and Star and all their friends watched the building of the room with great interest. They were also full of ideas and suggestions. Billy picked out a place that he thought would be perfect for a model railroad. When he pointed it out to Betsy, she said, "But we don't have a railroad."

"You ought to get one," said Billy.

Betsy wasn't interested, but when Ellen said, "Oh, Betsy! This place under the stairs would make a wonderful doll's house," Betsy was delighted.

"Why, Ellen!" she said. "It would! I'll ask Father to build us a doll's house under the stairs."

When Betsy asked her father to build a doll's house

17

under the stairs, he said, "Look, Betsy! I built a summerhouse for you, and I have just finished a winterhouse for you. If you want a doll's house, you'll have to build it yourself. There are plenty of scraps left over from the winterhouse for you. Get Billy to help you."

Billy was delighted to help build the dollhouse and he arrived for the job early on Saturday morning.

"Oh, Billy!" said Betsy. "I have the most wonderful thing for one of the walls. It's an old door with glass in the top." She led the way down to the basement. "If we put the door on its side," she said, "the glass part will make a lovely picture window."

"Sounds O.K.," said Billy.

Soon Ellen arrived. "What are you doing?" she asked, as she came down the stairs.

"We're building a doll's house," Betsy replied.

"Oh, good!" said Ellen. "Can I help?"

"Sure!" said Billy. "Come help us put this wall in place."

The three children carried the old door around to one side of the stairs. They rested it on its side and leaned it against the steps. "We'll have to drive some

nails through it to keep it steady," said Billy. "Is that O.K.?"

"Yes," replied Betsy. "Father said that we would have to put nails in. Do you know how to hammer nails in, Billy?"

"Sure, I do," replied Billy. "You two hold it steady."

"Be careful you don't break the picture window," said Betsy.

It took Billy a long time to hammer the first nail through the wooden door, but he finally made it hold. The next one was easier. "Now," he said, "what about the opposite wall?"

"Here's a big piece of wooden crisscross stuff," said Betsy. "I think it would fit."

"O.K.!" said Billy. "Let's try it."

"It will look like a cage," said Ellen.

"Oh, no, it won't," said Betsy. "If it were a cage there wouldn't be any crosspieces."

Betsy and Billy put the second wall in place. "Now, we'll just let it lean against the steps until we get the front up," said Billy.

"All right," said Betsy. "How about making the other wall out of these orange crates? We can put one on top of the other and nail them together."

"That's swell," said Billy. "They'll make shelves inside, and you can keep things in them."

20

Betsy and Ellen piled the orange crates one upon the other. Then Billy went inside and nailed them to the wall that had been a door. "Now, kids!" he called out. "Hold that other wall while I nail the crates to it." Betsy and Ellen held the lattice wall and Billy drove the nails in. "There!" he said. "That's good and tight."

Just then a voice called from outside, "Hey, Betsy!"

"Oh, that must be Kenny Roberts," said Betsy. "He said he might come over today."

Betsy ran to the stairs and called, "We're down in the basement, Kenny. Come on down."

Kenny soon appeared at the top of the stairs. "What are you doing?" he called down.

"We're building a doll's house under the stairs," Betsy called back. "Billy Porter is here. He's helping us."

Kenny came bounding down the steps. "Can I help build it too?" he asked.

"Hi, Ken!" Billy called out. "You're just in time to help put the roof on."

21

"Yes," said Betsy. "We have this other door to use for the roof. It's heavy, but if you will help Ellen and me lift it, Kenny, we can put it up."

"Sure!" said Kenny.

The three children lifted the old door and placed it across the walls of the house. "Now, I'll put some nails in to hold the roof in place," said Kenny.

"Here!" said Betsy. "If you stand on this stool, you can reach the top."

Betsy pushed a stool over beside the house. Ellen handed Kenny a hammer and some nails. Kenny put the nails in his pocket and climbed on top of the stool. While Kenny hammered nails, Betsy admired the roof. "It's nice the way it sticks out on both sides," she said.

"Oh, it's a wonderful roof," said Ellen.

"Sure makes it real cozy," said Billy from inside. Billy was going over every nail, hammering them in more securely. "Don't want it to fall apart," he said.

"That's right," said Kenny, banging on the roof.

"Look, Kenny," said Betsy, when Kenny climbed

off the stool, "look at the beautiful picture window on this side."

Kenny went around to the other side. "That's neat," he said. He examined the wall and said, "Needs a couple more nails here." He drove another nail into the door, fastening it more securely to the step. Then Kenny looked at the house from all sides. "Pretty neat," he said.

Billy was still hammering inside. "You should see the inside," said Billy. "These crates make swell shelves."

Kenny looked at the house all around. Then he said, "Hey! You forgot to put a door in it."

"Oh!" cried Betsy. "We forgot to put a door in it."

The hammering inside stopped. Then Billy said, "Well, say! How am I going to get out of here?"

"Oh, we can saw a door out of the lattice side," said Kenny. "Then you can crawl out."

"That's right," said Betsy. "We can saw a door out."

"Where's the saw, Betsy?" Kenny asked.

"Yes, where's the saw?" said Betsy, looking around. "Do you see the saw, Billy?"

"How can I see a saw from in here?" Billy asked. "Hurry up and find it. I want to get out of here. I'm thirsty."

"Ellen," said Betsy, "go get Billy a bottle of root beer out of the refrigerator."

Ellen went up to the kitchen and came back with a bottle of root beer. "Here it is," she said.

"Did you take the top off?" Billy asked.

"Oh, no!" Ellen replied.

"Well, how do you expect *me* to take the top off?" said Billy. "I guess you think I can do it with my teeth!"

Ellen went up to the kitchen again. When she returned, the top was off the bottle. "Here," she said, "I'll stick it through the lattice." Then in a moment she said, "Oh! It won't go through. It's too big."

"You're spilling it all over," said Billy. "Go get a straw."

"Now where do you suppose Father put his saw," Betsy muttered.

"Maybe it's in the garage," said Ellen.

"Sure is funny, we can't find the saw," said Kenny.

Billy began to yell, "Get a straw! Get a straw! Get a straw! I'm dying of thirst. Get a straw!"

"Where's a straw, Betsy?" asked Ellen.

"I don't think we have any," said Betsy. "Mother has gone to market, though. Maybe she'll bring some home with her."

"I'm thirsty," cried Billy. "I'm hungry, too."

"Now just wait a minute," said Betsy. "I'll get something for you to eat."

"Bring something that will go through these holes in this wall," said Billy.

"I guess I might as well drink this root beer," said Ellen. "All the bubbles are going out of it."

"Oh!" cried Billy. "Can't you find the saw?"

"Now, Billy," said Betsy, "do you want me to hunt for the saw or get you something to eat?"

"I want something to eat," replied Billy. "I'm starving."

"All right," said Betsy.

Betsy, Ellen, and Kenny went upstairs. They looked in the cooky jar. It was full of cookies, so they each took one. "Let's give Billy a cooky," said Ellen.

"They're too big," replied Betsy. "They would never go through one of those little holes."

"What about a peanut-butter sandwich?" asked Kenny.

"Too big," said Betsy. She opened the refrigerator door and the three children looked in.

"How about giving him a hot dog?" said Kenny. "That would go in."

"I'm not allowed to cook anything without asking my mother," said Betsy.

Billy began to hammer on the cellar stairs. "Hurry up!" he yelled. "Hurry up!"

Betsy called down to him, "We can't find anything small enough to go through the holes."

"You're eating something," Billy called back. "I hear you."

"We're eating cookies," said Betsy.

"Why don't you bring me a cooky?" Billy yelled.

"They're too big to go through," Betsy called back.

"Well, stupid! They break, don't they?" cried Billy.

"Oh, yes!" cried Betsy. "Of course!" She ran to the cooky jar, reached inside, and took out two cookies. Then Ellen took out two and Kenny took two. With their hands full of cookies they returned to the basement.

"It's about time!" said Billy.

"Father should be home soon," said Betsy. "He'll know where the saw is."

"Never mind the saw," said Billy. "Where are the cookies?"

The three children settled down and broke up the cookies. They fed the pieces to Billy through the holes in the lattice. In a few minutes Billy said, "These cookies are making me thirstier and thirstier."

"I have an idea," said Kenny. "Maybe we could fasten the hose for the garden on the faucet outside. Then we could bring the hose through the kitchen and down the cellar stairs and put the nozzle through one of these holes, and Billy could get a drink."

"Oh, I think that's a good idea," said Betsy.

Betsy, Ellen, and Kenny dashed up the stairs again. They found the garden hose in the garage. In a few minutes Kenny had it screwed on to the outdoor faucet. Betsy took hold of the nozzle, and Ellen helped her carry the hose through the kitchen door and down the cellar stairs. "It's coming, Billy," Betsy called to him.

"Oh, am I thirsty!" said Billy.

"Now, I'll put the nozzle right through one of these holes," said Betsy.

Betsy stuck the nozzle through one of the holes. As she did, Kenny turned on the water outside and the doll's house was suddenly turned into a shower bath. "Hey!" cried Billy. "Cut it out. Cut it out!"

30

"Kenny!" Betsy cried. "Shut it off."

"What's the matter?" said Ellen from the foot of the stairs.

"Tell Kenny to shut off the water," Betsy called back.

Just as the water was shut off, Betsy's father came home. "What's going on?" he said, when he saw the hose running through the kitchen and down the cellar stairs.

"We were giving Billy a drink of water," said Ellen.

"Isn't that a pretty fancy way to give Billy a drink of water?" said Betsy's father. "Where is he?"

"He's inside the dollhouse," said Ellen. "He's nailed in."

Betsy's father went down to the basement. "Oh, Father!" Betsy cried. "I'm so glad you came. Billy's inside the dollhouse, and we forgot to put a door in it. He was thirsty and we didn't have any straws, so we just had to bring the hose down."

"Yeah!" Billy called out. "And they soaked me."

31

"Now, Billy, we didn't mean to," said Betsy. "It was an accident." Then she said to her father, "Look, Father, could you cut a door right over here and let Billy out? We couldn't find the saw."

"I took the saw with me to have it sharpened," said Father.

Betsy's father began sawing the lattice wall. In a few minutes he had cut a piece out. Betsy and Ellen and Kenny watched as Billy crawled out of the opening. He looked as though he had been dipped in a swimming pool.

"Put on Betsy's raincoat, Billy," said Father. "Get right in the car, and I'll take you home."

Betsy ran to get her raincoat for Billy. "Good-by, Billy," she said, as he put on the raincoat. "Thanks for building my dollhouse."

"That's O.K.," said Billy.

As he climbed into the car he said, "Boy, am I thirsty!"

CHAPTER 2

CHRISTMAS CAROLS AND
THE BIRTHDAY TREE

IT WAS close to Christmas when Father had the winterhouse completed. By this time, Betsy's head was full of ideas for Christmas.

Star, Betsy's little sister, had two things to think about—Christmas and her birthday. Star had been born on Christmas Day, very early in the morning. So every year Star's birthday presents were always put under the Christmas tree with her Christmas presents. She always got them mixed up and kept asking all day long, "Is this a Christmas present or a birthday present?" Most people forgot about Star's birthday, because they were so busy thinking about Christmas. When they said, "Merry Christmas, Star," she would reply, "Merry Christmas to you." Then she would say, "Did you know it is my Happy Birthday, too?" Everyone would look a little bit ashamed, because they had forgotten Star's birthday, and they would say, "Oh, yes! So it is! Happy Birthday!"

One day Betsy was sitting at the desk Father had made for her down in the winterhouse. Star came and stood beside her. "What are you doing?" she asked her sister.

"I'm getting my Christmas cards ready to mail," replied Betsy. Betsy handed one of her cards to Star, so she could look at it.

"They're pretty," said Star.

"Yes," replied Betsy. "I always like Christmas cards that show people singing Christmas carols."

"Do they sing 'Happy Birthday'?" Star asked.

"Oh, no!" replied Betsy. "That isn't a Christmas carol."

"I don't see why they don't sing 'Happy Birthday,' " said Star. "It's the little Lord Jesus' birthday and it's my birthday."

"Well, they don't sing it," said Betsy. "I know, because we're learning Christmas carols at school."

"I know some," said Star. "Mother is teaching me."

"I'd like to go out on Christmas Eve and sing Christmas carols," said Betsy. "It would be fun to go over to Billy's house and stand outside and sing carols. He would be surprised."

"Can I go too?" asked Star.

"Oh, you're too little to go," replied Betsy.

"You couldn't go by yourself," said Star. "You couldn't sing loud enough all by yourself."

Betsy put her Christmas cards away in a box and

said, "Father likes to sing and he makes a great big noise when he sings. Let's go talk to Mother."

Betsy and Star went upstairs. They found Mother sitting beside the fire in the living room. She was letting down the hem of one of Betsy's dresses. "Mother," said Betsy, "can you and Father go with Star and me to sing Christmas carols on Christmas Eve?"

"Where do you want to go?" asked Mother.

"Just over to Billy Porter's house," replied Betsy. "We could stand outside and sing. It would be fun."

"What would be fun?" asked Father, coming into the room.

"We are all going caroling on Christmas Eve," said Mother.

"Caroling!" exclaimed Father. "I can't go out caroling on Christmas Eve. I have to trim the tree."

"Oh, I had forgotten about the Christmas tree," said Mother.

Betsy's face was sad. "Oh, dear," she sighed.

"How about going out before breakfast, early in the morning?" asked Father.

"Fine!" replied Mother.

"That's a good idea," said Betsy. "I read a story once about some people who went carol singing, and after they sang the people invited them inside, and they had refreshments. So maybe Billy Porter's mother will invite us to breakfast."

"Why, Betsy! Aren't you ashamed of yourself, trying to get a free breakfast," said her mother. "We always have good Christmas breakfasts here."

"Oh, but we don't have those big ginger cookies that Billy's grandmother bakes for them. Billy says they always have them on Christmas morning for breakfast."

Father interrupted. "Take your mind off cookies," he said. "Tell me where you want to have the Christmas tree this year. Do you want it here in the living room or downstairs in the winterhouse?"

"Oh, both!" cried Betsy.

"Can't have both," said Father. "One Christmas tree is enough."

"Oh, we must have it here!" said Mother. "It won't seem like Christmas if we can't open the front door and see the Christmas tree."

Suddenly Star spoke up. "Why aren't there birthday trees?" she asked.

"Birthday trees!" exclaimed Betsy. "Whoever heard of a birthday tree!"

"I think there should be birthday trees," said Star.

Star and Betsy went to bed early on Christmas Eve, and Father and Mother set to work trimming the tree. When they had finished they sat down to admire it. The tree stood on the floor and its top touched the ceiling. Only the lights on the tree were lit. The fireplace glowed with bright red embers. Father and Mother sat beside the fire, feeling its warmth.

In a few minutes, Mother said, "It's the prettiest tree we have ever had."

"You say that every year," said Father.

"It's true," said Mother. "Every year you are a better tree trimmer."

Father laughed. "What about the other tree?" he asked.

"Oh, yes!" replied Mother. "Let's get on with it."

Father put out the lights on the Christmas tree and went outside. In a few minutes he brought a small tree through the back door. "Come along," he said. "It won't take long to trim this one."

Father took the tree downstairs and into the children's winterhouse, and Mother followed him. Soon the tree was standing straight and firm in a corner of the room. They set to work again, and the tree grew more and more beautiful as they worked. Finally Mother draped a string of letters across the tree. She had made them herself and had painted them with gold paint. The letters said, *Happy Birthday to Star.*

"We'll put all of her birthday presents under this tree," said Mother. "This year Star won't get her

Christmas presents and birthday presents all mixed up." When the tree was finished, Mother placed seven packages under it. Then she and Father went to bed.

Very early in the morning, before daybreak, Betsy woke up. At first she did not know why she felt excited. Then, suddenly, she remembered. It was Christmas morning! She jumped out of bed and pulled on her bathrobe. She ran into Star's room. Star was sound asleep, so Betsy shook her shoulder. "Star!" she whispered. "Star! It's Christmas, Star!"

Star opened her eyes and said, "What?"

"It's Christmas!" said Betsy. "Get up! We're going out caroling. Don't you remember?"

Star rubbed her eyes and crawled out of bed, while Betsy went across the hall to Father and Mother's room. "Mother!" she called out. "Isn't it time to go caroling?"

Mother woke up and looked at the clock on the table beside her bed. It was four-thirty. "Yes, I guess so," she said.

Father just grunted and rolled over. Betsy shook him. "Father," she called. "Merry Christmas! It's time to go caroling."

Father grunted again. Then he said, "I can't sing this early in the morning." But he put his feet on the floor and sat on the edge of the bed. Then he yawned. "Whose idea was this to go caroling at this hour in the morning?"

"Yours," said Mother. Everyone laughed except Father. He just yawned again.

43

It wasn't long before Betsy and Star and their father and mother were in the car and on their way to Billy's house. It had begun to snow, and their car made the first tracks in the smooth white street.

"Billy is going to be surprised, isn't he?" said Star.

"Yes," said Betsy. "I hope they have those ginger cookies for breakfast."

When they reached Billy's house it was still dark, but as they drove into the driveway Father could see that the garage door was up and the car was gone. "They've gone out," he said. "The car is gone."

"Oh, no!" exclaimed Betsy. "Maybe they're home, anyway. Maybe somebody borrowed their car."

Betsy and Star and Father and Mother got out of the car. They tiptoed up the path to the front door. There was a beautiful wreath tied to the door knocker. Hanging from the wreath was a piece of white paper. Father struck a match and held it so that he could read what was written on the paper. He read it aloud. "Have gone caroling," it said.

"Oh, maybe they went to our house," said Betsy. "Let's hurry home."

"Listen," said Father, "you got me out of bed to sing Christmas carols and now I'm going to sing. If I can't sing to the Porters, I'll sing to their neighbors." Father opened his mouth and began to sing, "Hark, the herald angels sing." Betsy and Star and Mother joined in.

When they had finished, windows were opened and voices called out, "Merry Christmas! Merry Christmas!"

"Merry Christmas!" the carolers called back.

"Oh, I hope we haven't missed the Porters," said Betsy. "You think they'll come and sing for us, don't you, Mother?"

"I think they will," she replied.

"Do we have to go back to bed to listen?" asked Star.

"Oh, no!" said Mother. "Now that we're up, we'll stay up. I'll start breakfast so that we can invite them in."

"It's too bad about the ginger cookies," said Betsy.

When they reached home, the dawn was just breaking. A pinkish glow spread over the eastern sky. "Do you think they've been here already?" asked Betsy anxiously.

"There's no mark of tires in the snow, except ours," said Father.

"That's good," said Betsy.

"Now we will see our presents, won't we?" said Star.

"Yes," said Mother, as Father opened the front door.

The children ran into the living room without stopping to take off their coats and hats. As Father lit the tree, they both cried out, "Oh! Oh!"

"Oh! It's beautiful!" said Betsy.

Star was already on the floor looking over the packages under the tree.

"Your packages have a big *S* on them, Star," said her mother.

"And mine have a *B,*" said Betsy.

46

"Which are my birthday presents?" said Star. "How do I know which are my birthday presents?"

"Your birthday presents are not there," said Mother.

"Didn't I get any birthday presents?" Star cried.

"Of course you did," replied Mother. "They're down in the winterhouse. It's Christmas up here and birthday down there."

"Oh! Let's go see," said Betsy.

The children hurried downstairs. Father had already snapped on the lights. There stood the little tree, hung with nothing but stars and the gold letters.

"Why, it's Star's birthday tree!" cried Betsy.

"Oh!" cried Star. "I've got a birthday tree." She jumped up and down and shouted. "A birthday tree! A birthday tree!"

Just then Father put up his hand and said, "Listen!"

The children stood beside each other, listening. Voices came from outside. They were singing, "Silent Night." Betsy turned to run upstairs. Father put his arm around her and held her back. "Wait until they have finished," he said.

The two little girls stood clinging to Father as they listened to the familiar Christmas carols. Finally they heard something that surprised everyone except Star. The carolers were singing:

> Happy birthday to you,
> Happy birthday to you,
> Happy birthday, dear Star,
> Happy birthday to you.

Then they called out, "Merry Christmas!"

Betsy, Star, and Father rushed upstairs. Mother was already at the front door. "Merry Christmas!" she called out. "Come in. Come in."

Mr. and Mrs. Porter and Billy, with Ellen and Linda and their big brother, came into the house. They were all covered with snowflakes. Everyone called out, "Merry Christmas!"

"Star, did you hear us singing 'Happy Birthday'?" said Linda.

"Yes," said Star, her face shining.

"We each brought you a birthday present," said Ellen.

Star was delighted when she saw the packages. "Oh, thank you!" she cried. Then she said, "I have a birthday tree. It has me all over it."

"What do you mean, it has you all over it?" asked Billy.

"It has stars all over it," said Star. Everyone laughed.

"Here, Betsy," said Billy. "We brought you some ginger cookies."

"Oh, thank you!" said Betsy. "That's wonderful!"

Soon everyone was seated around the breakfast table. "Star," said Mother, "will you say grace?"

"Couldn't I sing a Christmas carol instead?" asked Star.

"Very well," said Mother. "Sing a Christmas carol."

Star looked around the table and everyone looked at Star. Then she bowed her head and sang:

> Happy birthday to you,
> Happy birthday to you,
> Happy birthday, Lord Jesus,
> Happy birthday to you.

CHAPTER 3

THE NEW YEAR CAKES

THE week between Christmas and New Year's Day was a happy one for Betsy and Star. There were new dolls to play with, new dresses to wear, new books to read, and new games to play. All during the week Betsy looked forward to New Year's Day, for she was having a party. She had invited ten of her friends from school.

On New Year's morning Betsy's mother got out her

electric cake mixer. She brought her biggest cake pans out of the closet. Soon the kitchen table was covered with all of the ingredients for a cake.

Betsy came into the kitchen and said, "Oh, Mother! What kind of cake are you going to make for the party?"

"A yellow cake with strawberry icing," replied her mother.

"That's my favorite kind," said Betsy. "Will it have three layers?"

"Yes," replied Mother. "We need a big cake. I'm going to make a few cupcakes, too."

"I'll get out the cupcake pans," said Betsy, opening the closet door.

"Put these paper cups into the pans," said Mother.

Betsy took the paper cups out of her mother's hand. While Mother sifted the flour and sugar together, Betsy lined each of the little molds with a paper cup. "Will twelve cupcakes be enough?" Betsy asked.

"Yes," replied Mother. "I want to do something special with them, and twelve is just the right number."

"What are you going to do that's special?" asked Betsy.

"Just wait and see," said Mother.

Soon the mixer was spinning the golden batter around and around in the bowl. When the batter was well mixed, Mother poured most of it into the three cake pans. The rest went into the twelve paper cups.

Star and Betsy licked the batter off the beaters. "Um-m!" said Star. "This is good."

"It's wonderful!" said Betsy. "And the cake will be even better."

Mother mixed up the strawberry icing and set the bowl aside. Soon the kitchen was filled with the delicious odor of baking cake. When Betsy and Star had finished with the beaters, they placed them in the sink. Then they went outdoors to play in the snow.

In about half an hour the cakes were done. Mother took them out of the oven. The three large cakes she turned out of the pans onto a clean white towel. The cupcakes, still in their paper cups, she lifted out. Then she set all of the cakes aside to cool.

Mother went downstairs to see if she could help Father. He was getting the winterhouse ready for the party. He had put up a long folding table and covered it with a white cloth. Now he was fastening pink crepe paper around the edge. It hung down and made a pink apron around the table. "What time is this party?" asked Father.

"At four o'clock," replied Mother.

"What are they going to do at the party?" Father asked.

"Oh, play games," replied Mother, "and, of course, eat. Ice cream and cake, candy and nuts."

After a while, Mother went back to the kitchen to ice her cakes.

She looked at the three big cakes and said to herself, "They are cool enough to ice now." She picked up the cake for the bottom layer and placed it on a large cake plate. Then she spread some of the strawberry icing over it.

Suddenly, the telephone rang. As Mother went into the hall to answer the telephone, Thumpy, Betsy's cocker spaniel, trotted upstairs from the basement. He sniffed the odor of cake. Thumpy liked cake. In fact, he liked it very much.

Thumpy walked around the kitchen table with his nose pointing upward. Sniff! Sniff! Sniff! Then he jumped on a nearby chair. Now he had a good view of the cakes. His nose twitched. Sniff! Sniff! Sniff! Bang! Bang! Bang! went Father's hammer in the basement. "Happy New Year!" Mother called into the telephone.

Thumpy put his front paws on the edge of the table. He stretched his neck out until his nose reached the nearest big cake. It was not a cupcake; it was one of the layers. He took a big sniff and then he took a big bite. He gobbled it down. Then he heard footsteps in the hall, and he jumped down and ran for the cellar stairs. He was gone when Betsy's mother returned.

It didn't take Mother a minute to see what had happened, and she knew at once who had bitten a piece out of the cake. "Oh, Thumpy!" she cried. Then she called downstairs, "Is Thumpy down there?"

"Yes, he's here," Father called back. "He has just gone under the sofa. What did he do?"

"Oh, dear!" said Mother. "He ruined one of the cakes. He bit a piece out of it."

Just then Betsy and Star came in through the back door. "Look!" said Mother to Betsy. "Just look what Thumpy did."

"Oh, Mother!" exclaimed Betsy. "What will you do now?"

"I can't bake another cake," replied Mother. "I only have time to put the icing on these." She picked up a knife and cut a large pie-shaped slice out of the cake where Thumpy had bit into it.

"Can I eat that?" asked Star.

"No," replied her mother. "This is where Thumpy bit into it. I have to throw this piece away." After she threw the piece away, she picked up the remainder of the layer and placed it on top of the bottom layer.

"It looks as though it had a tooth out," said Betsy.

"It certainly does," said Mother.

"Maybe you could put something in there so that when you ice it, the hole won't show," said Betsy.

"That's an idea," said Mother. "Now, what can we use?" Mother looked around the kitchen. She didn't see anything. "There must be something here that will hold up the top layer," she said.

Betsy pulled open a drawer. She picked up a square yellow sponge, wrapped in cellophane. "Look!" she cried, holding it up. "Maybe you could use a piece of this. It looks something like cake and it's even the same color."

Mother took the sponge out of Betsy's hand. "Why, Betsy!" she cried. "It's the very thing!"

Betsy pulled off the cellophane. "It's just as thick as

the cake," she said. In a moment a wedge of sponge was neatly fitted into the space in the cake.

"I hope I don't get that piece," said Star, as she watched her mother cover the cake with the icing.

"We must be sure that no one gets it," said Mother. "I'll put a toothpick in, so we'll know which piece must stay on the plate."

"No one will ever know, will they?" said Star.

"Not when the sides are covered with the icing," replied Mother, as she placed the third layer on top. When the cake was finished, it looked perfect. Mother placed it on the top of the stove. "Now," she said, "Thumpy *can't* jump up there!"

Betsy and Star went down to the winterhouse to see what Father was doing.

Mother iced the twelve cupcakes. When they were finished, she mixed up some white icing. With the white icing, she made a letter on the top of each little cake. She made two with the letter *A*, two with an *E*, two *P's,* and two *Y's*. She made an *R,* an *N,* a *W,* and an *H.* When they were finished, she put the plate of cupcakes on the window sill. Then she went upstairs to write some letters.

When Father finished decorating the winterhouse, it looked very gay. Crepe paper in every color of the rainbow was strung across the ceiling, from corner to corner.

Father came up to the kitchen followed by Star. He stopped by the stove and looked at the big cake. He turned it around to admire it and knocked the toothpick out. He picked the toothpick up and stuck it back in the side of the cake, wondering what it was for. Of course, he thought he stuck it back where it had been. Then he looked over the cupcakes on the window sill. "Oh!" he said. "I guess these are for us."

Father looked at them more closely. "They have letters on them," he said. "Now what do you know about that! Your mother certainly likes to fool around when she cooks. Well, there seem to be two *Y's.* I guess I can eat a *Y.*" He picked up a cupcake with a *Y* on it and ate it. "Very good!" he said. Then he held the plate out to Star and said, "Do you want one, Star?"

"Which one shall I take?" Star asked.

"Better take an *A*," said Father. "There seem to be two *A's*."

Star looked at the plate of cupcakes. Then she said, "I think I would like this one." She picked up the cupcake with an *N* on it.

"Oh, I don't know whether you should take that one," said Father. "There's only one *N*." But Star had already taken a bite out of the cake.

Later Betsy came upstairs. She went through the kitchen without stopping to look at the cakes, and up to her room to dress for the party.

About half past three Mother and Betsy came downstairs. Betsy was wearing a red velveteen dress that had been a Christmas present and a full petticoat underneath. She followed Mother into the kitchen. "Betsy," said her mother, "take those cupcakes down to the winterhouse and decorate the center of the table with them. You'll find that they spell out a message."

"They do!" cried Betsy. "Oh, Mother! That was your secret about the cupcakes, wasn't it?"

Mother laughed. "Yes," she replied.

Betsy carried the plate of cakes very carefully. She placed it on the table and then looked over the cakes. It did not take her long to see that she could make the word *Happy*. She set the letters out in the center of the table and put each cake on a paper doily. "I know what the message is," Betsy said with a chuckle to herself. She looked for a cake with an *N* on it, but she was surprised to find that there was no *N*. So she made the word *We*. Now there were only three letters left, an *E*, an *A*, and an *R*. She looked down at them and saw that they spelled the word *Ear*.

"Happy we ear!" muttered Betsy. "That doesn't make any sense." Then she placed the *R* between the *E* and the *A*, and read, *Happy We Era*. "That's crazy!" said Betsy, and she shifted the letters again. This time she put the *A* where the *E* was and the *E* where the *A* was, and read, *Happy We Are.* "Well, that's true," said Betsy to herself, "but it's a funny kind of message to put on the table."

Just then Mother came in. She looked at the table and said, "Betsy! Where are the other two cupcakes that I made?"

"These are all the cupcakes that were on the plate," said Betsy.

"But the message was to be, *Happy New Year,*" said her mother. "There's a *Y* and an *N* missing."

"Oh! I'm sure I didn't drop any," said Betsy.

"I know. I know what happened," said Mother. "It's that Thumpy again."

Thumpy hid under the sofa once more, although he didn't know what he had done this time.

By four o'clock all of Betsy's guests had arrived. Each one looked at the cupcakes and read, *Happy We Are,* and each one thought it was very true. They were always happy to be at a party.

Billy was the only one who counted the cupcakes.

He counted the children, too. "Hey, Betsy!" he said. "There aren't enough cupcakes to go 'round."

"Oh, we have a great big cake, too, Billy," said Betsy.

The children played games until five o'clock. The winterhouse rang with their shouting and laughing. At five o'clock Betsy's mother came in with the big cake. She had cut it into pie-shaped pieces. Maggie, the laundress, had come to help. She carried a tray with dishes of ice cream on it. She placed them around the table with a plate beside each dish for a slice of cake. There was a fork and spoon beside each plate. "Come, children!" said Betsy's mother. "Come sit down and have your ice cream and cake."

The children gathered around the table. Chairs scraped on the floor. The girls' dresses rustled as they sat down. A few of the boys remembered to pull up their trousers, so that they wouldn't get baggy at the knees. They all picked up their spoons and began eating their ice cream.

Maggie moved around the table, placing slices of cake on the plates. Betsy's mother had told her to watch out for the toothpick. The piece it was on, she had told her, was to remain on the plate. Maggie was careful.

"That sure looks like good cake," said Billy. He looked at his slice, standing up straight, one layer on top of the other. He picked up his fork and cut down through the pink icing and down through the first layer. Then he hit the second layer. He pressed down

68

but the fork didn't go through. Instead, this layer just bent down and, as it bent down, the back end rose up. The top layer flew forward and landed, icing side down, on Billy's lap.

Billy picked it up and put it back where it belonged. Then he wiped the strawberry icing off his suit with his napkin. He went back to work on the cake. Again he pressed his fork down on the second layer. The front end bent down, the back rose up, and the top layer flew in the air. This time it landed on Mary Lou's plate beside Billy's.

"Oh, thanks, Billy!" said Mary Lou. "Don't you like your cake?"

Before Billy could say anything, Mary Lou was eating his top layer of cake. He decided to give up the fork. He picked up the middle layer and put it into his mouth. He bit. All he could do was pinch the cake. When he opened his mouth everything was just the same. He couldn't bite a piece off no matter how hard he tried.

69

Billy put the slice back on his plate and went to work on the bottom layer. It was very good. When he had finished it, Mary Lou looked at the middle layer that was left on Billy's plate and said, "Why, Billy! Don't you want that piece of cake?"

"No," said Billy. "You can have it."

Mary Lou picked up the piece of cake, stuck it into her mouth, and clamped her teeth down. Billy watched her. "Good?" he asked.

"What's the matter with this piece of cake?" Mary Lou cried out.

"Oh, Mary Lou!" said Betsy's mother. "I am so sorry! You must have got the piece of cake with the sponge in it! Here, have another piece."

Betsy's mother came to Mary Lou and placed another whole piece of cake on her plate. Mary Lou went right to work on it. Billy watched her. As soon as Betsy's mother had moved away, Billy said, "Mary Lou, you are a pig."

Mary Lou burst into tears. She pushed her plate

away, got up, shook her petticoats, and rushed up-stairs. Billy finished up Mary Lou's cake. By the time the party was all over, however, Mary Lou had returned to the winterhouse. The signs of tears had disappeared.

When Billy said good-by to Betsy's mother, he said, "You don't mind if I take this piece of cake home to my mother, do you? She likes this stuff to wash the dishes." He held up the center layer.

Betsy's mother laughed. "Take it along, Billy," she said.

When everyone had gone home, Betsy and Star and Father and Mother sat in the living room around the Christmas tree. "If Thumpy hadn't eaten those two cupcakes," said Mother, "there would have been a cupcake for you, Betsy, and one for Star."

"Oh!" cried Father. "Thumpy didn't eat the cupcakes. Star and I ate them."

"Poor Thumpy!" said Betsy. "He gets blamed for everything."

"Well, he did eat part of the layer cake," said Mother.

"Never mind," said Father. "It has been a Happy New Year and *happy we are.*"

CHAPTER 4

LINDA'S DREAM CAT

IT WAS Friday night. Betsy and her little sister Star had invited Ellen and Linda to spend the week end with them. Linda was Ellen's little sister. Linda never let Star forget that she was two years older, but Star was always glad to have Linda come to play with her. "Linda bosses me," Star would occasionally complain.

"You shouldn't let her," Betsy would remark.

But when Star said, "How?" Betsy didn't know the answer, and Star really did not care. She was very fond of Linda, and things always happened when Linda was around. Star had noticed that when she tried to boss Linda, nothing happened. But when Linda did the bossing, Star soon found herself in the middle of something exciting.

Ellen had seen how things were with Linda even before Linda could talk. She had seen how things were the day Linda, sitting in her high chair, had tried on her full bowl of oatmeal as a hat. Ellen had formed the habit of saying, "Now, Linda, do be careful."

Linda always opened her eyes very wide and replied, "I am!" This made Ellen wonder what things would be like if Linda wasn't careful.

Now Linda was sleeping peacefully in the upper bunk bed above Star. Over Linda's head, rain beat down on the roof. It beat so hard that the noise wakened Linda. At first she didn't know where she was, but when she sat up and looked around, she remembered that Star was down below and Ellen and Betsy were in the next room.

Just then Linda heard a cat meow. She listened. She thought of her own big gray tomcat, Tobey. The cat meowed louder and the rain beat down harder. Linda listened and wondered whether it was Tobey. Perhaps he was looking for her. Linda had heard of cats that walked miles and miles to find their owners. Poor Tobey, thought Linda.

Finally Linda decided to get up and see if it really was Tobey. In the dark, she felt for the ladder that led down to the floor. Then she crawled backward to the edge of the bunk and dangled her leg over until her foot touched one of the rungs of the ladder. Without making a sound she climbed down. There was a night light burning near the floor, so Linda could see her way to the door. There was a little light in the hall, too, so Linda found her way to the back stairs. She ran down the steps and pushed open the door at the bottom that led into the kitchen.

75

Linda could still hear the cat meowing. It was louder now. She thought it must be right by the back door. She opened the door a crack and whispered, "Is that you, Tobey?"

There was no reply, just the sound of the rain beat-

ing on the driveway. "Here, pussy! Pussy!" Linda whispered.

Suddenly she jumped. A soft furry body had skimmed past her leg. The cat was inside! Linda closed the door. The cat rubbed against her and made the bottom of her nightgown wet. She reached down and stroked it. The cat felt very wet. A little daylight began to appear now, and in the dim light Linda could see that it was not Tobey. This cat wasn't as big as Tobey.

Linda didn't want to put the cat out in the rain again. It would just get wetter and cry louder, she thought. Then she had another idea. She opened the cellar door and gave the cat a gentle push. The cat went down the cellar stairs. She closed the door and went back up the stairs. She opened the door of the bedroom very quietly and tiptoed across the floor. She climbed back into her bunk. Soon she was sound asleep.

When the children came down to breakfast, Linda went right down to the cellar. At first no one missed her, but when everyone was seated at the table, Betsy's mother said, "Where's Linda?"

Ellen called out, "Linda! Linda! Where are you?"

A muffled answer came from beneath the dining-room floor. "I'm down here."

Betsy ran to the cellar door and opened it. "Linda!" she called. "Breakfast is ready. What are you doing?"

"I'm looking for the cat," Linda replied. "I can't find it."

"We haven't any cat, silly," said Betsy, as Linda climbed the cellar stairs.

"There was a cat," said Linda.

"When was there a cat?" asked Star, as Linda sat down to breakfast beside Ellen.

"Last night there was a cat," said Linda.

"You were dreaming," said Ellen.

"Well, I thought it was real," said Linda.

Star laughed. "Linda thought the cat she was dreaming about was real."

78

"It was wet," said Linda, swallowing her first spoonful of cereal.

Thumpy, Betsy's cocker spaniel, seemed excited about something. He couldn't settle down for a minute. He kept running back and forth, sniffing here and sniffing there, and especially sniffing in the kitchen.

"What's the matter with Thumpy this morning?" exclaimed Betsy's mother.

"Maybe he smells the cat," said Linda.

The rest of the children laughed. "Thumpy smells the cat that Linda dreamed about," said Betsy.

"Linda's so funny!" cried Star.

After breakfast the sun came out and the children played outdoors. Linda forgot about the cat. In the middle of the afternoon Billy Porter arrived. He came inside and stood at the foot of the stairs. He called up, "Hey, Betsy!"

"Hello, Billy!" Betsy called back, running to the top of the stairs. "Come on up. Ellen and Linda are here."

But Billy had pressing business. "Say, Betsy," he said, "you know that little can of blue paint you had down in the basement?"

"I know," replied Betsy.

"Well, can I go down and paint this little boat with that can of paint?" Billy held up a small sailboat. "I brought my own brush."

"Of course you can," said Betsy. "Go ahead down. We'll all be down in a minute."

Billy went through the dining room and into the kitchen. He opened the cellar door and went down the steps. He passed through the laundry and opened the door on which Betsy had painted *Winterhouse* in blue letters. He forgot to shut the door. There were cans of paint, modeling clay, a package of Easter-egg dyes, some stencils, and a model of a little house.

Billy soon picked out the can of blue paint. He carried it to Betsy's worktable and pried off the lid. With the handle of an old paintbrush he stirred the paint. He was thinking what a pretty shade of blue the paint was when he heard a strange sound. Billy stopped stirring the paint and listened. There was the sound again. It's a cat, thought Billy.

Billy put down the brush and looked around. He didn't see any cat so he returned to the can of paint. Then in a moment he heard the sound again. It seemed to come from the laundry, and Billy walked in. The door of the washing machine had been left open, so that it hung out like a shelf. There was the sound again. Billy stooped down and looked inside the washing machine. To his great surprise, there, inside, was a tortoise-shell cat and two kittens.

Billy ran to the foot of the basement stairs. "Hey, Betsy!" he called. "Betsy!" He could hear Betsy's feet running across the floor overhead. "Betsy!" he cried again.

Betsy opened the door. "What is it?" she called out.

"Hey, Betsy! Did you know that your cat has kittens?" Billy called back.

"We don't have a cat," said Betsy.

81

"Well, there's a cat down here with kittens," said Billy.

Betsy started down the stairs but Thumpy pushed ahead. "Where are they?" she asked in a very surprised voice.

"In the washing machine," said Billy.

Now Thumpy was barking furiously. He rushed to the washing machine and jumped about. The noise brought Star and Ellen and Linda to the head of the stairs. "What's the matter?" Ellen called out.

"There's a cat with kittens in the washing machine," Billy shouted back.

Ellen, Star, and Linda started down the stairs. "Are they really in the washing machine?" said Ellen.

"Sure," replied Billy. "Come see."

The children crowded around and peered inside the washer. Thumpy acted like a wild animal. "Be quiet, Thumpy," said Betsy.

"You'll scare the cat to death, Thumpy," said Billy.

Betsy took hold of Thumpy's collar and dragged

him to the foot of the stairs. Then she boosted him up the steps.

All the children were talking at once. "Aren't they sweet little kittens?" said Star.

"Their eyes aren't open yet," said Billy.

"They're so cute," said Ellen. "I never saw such tiny ones before."

"I never saw yellow kittens before," said Linda. "I've only seen gray ones."

"That's because the mother is a tortoise-shell cat," said Betsy. "The kittens are going to be like the mother. I wonder whose cat it is."

"Well, Betsy," said Billy. "If this cat isn't your cat, I think these kittens should be mine, because I found them."

"No, Billy!" said Star. "They're ours, because they got born in our washing machine."

"Oh, no!" Linda cried out. "They're mine, because I saw the cat first."

"What do you mean, you saw it first?" said Billy.

"You didn't even know about it till I showed you."

"Yes, I did too," said Linda. " 'Cause I let the cat in the back door."

Everyone turned from the cat and the kittens and looked at Linda. "That was a dream cat," said Star.

Linda threw back her head, opened her mouth, and yelled. "It was not. It was not a dream cat. It was real, and now it has kittens. And they are all mine."

The noise in the basement brought Betsy's mother downstairs. "What's the matter?" she asked.

"Oh, Mother!" said Betsy. "There's a cat with two kittens in the washing machine."

"And Linda says the kittens are hers, just because she dreamed about a cat last night," said Star.

Linda was crying louder than ever now. Her face was wet with tears.

Betsy's mother leaned over and looked at the cat and the kittens. "How did they ever get in there?" she said.

Linda continued to sob. "I didn't dream it. I didn't dream it," she cried.

Betsy's mother put her arm around Linda and said, "Come, Linda, tell me all about it." She led Linda to a bench and they sat down. While the rest of the children chattered around the washing machine, Linda told her story about letting the cat in to Betsy's mother. Her tears dried as she talked. When she finished she said, "Ellen and Betsy and Star don't believe that it was a real cat. But you believe me, don't you?"

"Yes, Linda," said Betsy's mother. "I believe you."

"So the kittens are mine, aren't they?" said Linda.

"No, darling," said Mother. "The kittens belong to the cat and the cat belongs to somebody, and we must try to find the somebody who owns the cat. Meanwhile, we must take them out of the washing machine and put them in a box."

Soon a box was found, and Betsy's mother lifted the kittens out of the washing machine and placed them in the box. Then the cat jumped out and followed her kittens.

"Now," said Betsy's mother, "we must find out who owns the cat."

Linda looked up from where she was kneeling beside the box. "Can I make believe the kittens are mine?" she asked.

"No!" shouted all the other children in a chorus.

"Well, it was a real cat, anyhow," said Linda. "A dream cat couldn't have kittens, could it, Ellen?"

"Sure, if you dreamed a cat had kittens, then a dream cat would have dream kittens," said Billy.

"But these are real kittens," said Linda. "These aren't dream kittens. Anybody can see that they're real."

"Sure, sure," said Billy. "They're real."

"They're real cute," said Ellen.

"They're real pretty," said Star.

"And now we have to find out the real owner," said Betsy.

All the children laughed. Billy picked up his boat and started to paint.

CHAPTER 5

A NAME FOR A LADY CAT

WHILE Billy painted his boat, the girls chattered about the cat and the kittens. "We should name the kittens," said Star.

"We don't even know what the mother's name is," said Linda.

"Those kittens should have good washing-machine names," said Billy.

"Washing-machine names!" exclaimed Linda. "What is a washing-machine name?"

"Why, like Soapsuds," said Billy.

The children laughed. "We could name one Soapie and the other Sudsie," said Betsy.

"Oh, that's good!" Ellen cried. "Let's decide which one is Soapie and which is Sudsie."

The children leaned over the box and examined the kittens. "I think the all-yellow one should be Soapie," said Billy. "It's just the same color as the yellow soap my father uses to wash his paintbrushes."

"Well, then the other one is Sudsie," said Betsy.

"And that's good, too," said Ellen, "because it has some white on it and it looks liks soapsuds." Everyone was happy with the names for the kittens.

Now the children began to sniff the odor of chocolate brownies baking. Billy put his boat on a shelf to dry and led the way upstairs. Betsy's mother had just taken a pan of brownies out of the oven. She was putting them on a towel to cool.

"Oh, brownies!" Star cried.

"Yes!" said her mother. "When they're cool you can each have one with a glass of milk. Put on your coats and go outside to play. The cat and the kittens need to be quiet. When it's time to eat the brownies, I'll call you."

The children put on their coats and jackets. It was March and still cold, even though the sun was shining brightly.

Outside, Betsy said, "We should try to find the person who owns the cat. I guess they're looking everywhere for it."

"Well, let's ask everybody we meet if they lost a cat," said Ellen.

"I don't want to," cried Linda. "They will take the kittens. I won't go."

"Then we'll go without you," said Ellen. Linda came along but she pouted.

The children had not gone far when they met a boy about Linda's age. He had taken his cap off. His head was covered with thick hair the color of a carrot. He was sucking a lollipop. Betsy had never seen the boy in the neighborhood before. "Hello!" she called to him.

The boy took his lollipop out of his mouth, and said, "Hi!"

"What's your name?" said Star.

"I won't tell you," replied the boy, and licked his lollipop.

"We found a cat in our washing machine," said Star. Before she could add, "with two kittens," the little boy's name popped out of him like a cork out of a popgun.

"My name's Ralph," he said. Then he quickly added, "I lost my cat."

"You did!" cried Betsy. "Where do you live?"

Ralph pointed to a house down the street that had a sign on it, *Sold.* "We just moved in there yesterday," he said. "I lost my cat."

"Oh! It's his cat. I bet it's his cat, for sure," said Billy.

"Well, never mind," said Betsy. "We have it and we'll give it back to you, Ralph."

"And what do you think!" Billy cried. Before Ralph could say what he thought, Billy said, "There are two kittens that come with it."

Ralph's face lit up like the sun. "Two kittens!"

"They have names," said Star. "Soapie and Sudsie."

Linda's face was very sad. "Maybe you won't like the kittens," she said. "They're yellow."

"Oh, I'll like 'em fine," said Ralph. "I like any color kittens. Pink or green or purple, or any color."

"There are no pink or green or purple kittens," said Linda. "Are there, Ellen?"

"I mean if there were I would like 'em," said Ralph.

"Come on back to my house and see them," said Betsy.

The children led Ralph back to Betsy's house. They all trooped into the kitchen through the back door. Betsy's mother looked surprised. "I told you that I would call you," she said.

"I know, Mother," said Betsy. "But we found the little boy who owns the cat. This is Ralph."

"He just moved here," said Star. "He doesn't live very far away."

"He shouldn't get the kittens, should he?" said Linda. "They were born in this house, and I don't think he should get them."

"But it's his cat," said Betsy. "The kittens belong to his cat, so that makes the kittens his." Ralph just stood and licked his lollipop.

"Come on, Ralph," said Billy. "Come on down to the cellar and see the kittens. They're cute."

"Now, children!" said Betsy's mother. "Don't touch the cat or the kittens. They must be kept quiet for a while."

"Oh, we'll be very quiet," said Betsy.

Billy led the way and the five other children followed. They went on tiptoe. Linda was at the end of the line. She did not tiptoe. She dragged her feet and her lower lip stuck out.

"There is the washing machine they were born in," Star whispered, as she pointed to the washer.

"And here they are!" exclaimed Billy, forgetting to whisper.

Billy lifted the cloth. Ralph leaned over and looked into the box. "Oh!" he exclaimed.

The children waited for Ralph to say something more than "Oh," but that was all he said. "Oh!"

"What's your cat's name?" asked Betsy.

Ralph took his lollipop out of his mouth and said, "Peter."

"Peter!" exclaimed all of the children.

"Whoever heard of a lady named Peter!" cried Linda.

"I guess, Ralph, you didn't know she was a lady cat?" said Betsy.

"Well, you will have to give her another name, Ralphie," said Billy.

"Oh, yes!" said Ellen. "You can't call the mother of kittens Peter."

"Name's Peter," said Ralph, not bothering to remove the lollipop.

Betsy paid no attention to what Ralph had said. Instead, she called out, "Now everybody think of a good name instead of Peter."

"I think it should be something like Peter, because if you suddenly begin calling a cat named Peter, Mildred, it won't know that you're calling it at all," said Ellen.

"Wouldn't call my cat Mildred," said Ralph.

"Nobody wants you to call your cat Mildred," said Betsy.

"She said Mildred," said Ralph, pointing with his lollipop to Ellen.

"She wasn't saying it for real," said Betsy. "She just said, 'A name like Mildred.' "

"Name's Peter," said Ralph.

"How would Peterkin be?" asked Ellen.

"No!" said Billy. "That means little Peter. It would still be a boy cat."

"But it can't be a boy cat, Billy," said Linda. "If it was a boy cat, it couldn't have kittens."

"I know that, silly," said Billy. "I just said, if its name was Peterkin it would have to be a boy cat."

"Well, now! Let's all think," said Ellen.

Betsy, Ellen, Star, and Linda wrinkled up their foreheads and thought. Billy scratched his head. Ralph knelt beside the box and looked at the kittens. Finally Betsy said, "How about Peterette?"

"Sounds like something you wear," said Billy. "Like an undershirt or something."

The children thought some more. In a few moments Ellen said, "Oh! I know a good one."

Everyone but Ralph looked at Ellen. "What is it?" Betsy asked.

Ellen looked very pleased with herself. "Petrella!" she said.

"Oh, that's wonderful!" Betsy cried. "It couldn't be better! Petrella!"

"Sounds like something from a medicine bottle,"

said Billy. "Petrella! For that bad cough, take Petrella."

"Oh, Billy!" cried Betsy. "I think you're terrible. You didn't think of any name at all. I think Petrella is a lovely name. Now come on, I think we should christen the cat Petrella, and that will make it sure."

"You can't christen a cat with water," said Ellen, "because cats don't like water."

"Well, they like milk," said Billy. "We could christen her with a few drops of milk."

"I know they like milk in their stomachs," said Ellen, "but I don't know whether they like milk on their heads. Milk on your head would feel just like water on your head."

"We'll show it to her first," said Billy.

Betsy looked in the box to see if the cat had drunk all the milk she had given her. The saucer was empty. "I'll go upstairs and get some more milk," she said. "Now don't make any noise. Remember, they have to be kept quiet."

Betsy went up to the kitchen. "We have to have a little milk for the cat," she said to her mother. "We are naming her Petrella."

Soon Betsy returned, carrying the saucer of milk. She carried it very carefully. "Now, I'll just drop a few drops and, Ellen, you say, 'I christen thee Petrella.'"

Just as Betsy held the dish of milk over the box, Ralph got up suddenly. His head bumped Betsy's arm and the whole saucer of milk spilled over the cat and splashed on the kittens. "Meow!" said the cat.

"I christen you Petrella!" said Ellen very quickly.

"Ellen didn't say it right," said Star. "She didn't say *thee*."

"I want to take 'em home," said Ralph.

"Oh, I don't think you should move them yet," said Betsy.

"You shouldn't have poured that milk into the box," said Ralph. "You should have put the dish in the box."

"I didn't mean to pour the milk into the box," said

Betsy. "You joggled me. We were just christening your cat Petrella."

"Name's Peter," said Ralph.

"Ralph!" exclaimed Betsy. "You can't call her Peter now, because we have just this minute christened her Petrella."

At this moment Betsy's mother called down the stairs, "Come up, children. Here are your milk and brownies." There was a wild dash to the kitchen.

The cat quietly licked the milk off herself and her babies.

The children stood around the table, eating their brownies and drinking their milk. "Mother," said Betsy, "Ralph wants to take Petrella and the kittens to his house. Is it all right for him to take them now?"

"I'll bring the box upstairs and put it in your express wagon, but you must wheel them home without shaking them up," replied her mother.

"We'll be very careful," said Betsy.

"Ralph," said Linda, "won't you give me one of the kittens?"

Ralph shook his head. "No," he said. "I like kittens." Linda's lower lip came out and tears filled her eyes.

When the milk glasses were empty and every crumb had been eaten, the children put on their coats and sweaters. Betsy led the way to the garage. She pulled out the express wagon. "We'll come with you, Ralph," she said.

Betsy's mother brought the box and placed it in the wagon. The cat and the kittens were covered up with a piece of an old blanket. The procession started off. Ralph pulled the wagon and Betsy steadied the box. At the curbs Billy lifted up the back end of the wagon, so that the box would not be bumped.

When they reached Ralph's house, they halted. Billy and Ralph picked up the box. The girls stayed with the wagon. " 'By now!" said Ralph. Billy and Ralph carried the box around to the back of the house.

"Well!" exclaimed Betsy, as she waited with the others for Billy to return. "He never even said thank-you."

"After we found his cat and gave him the kittens," said Ellen.

"And you thought of that beautiful name and christened his cat," said Betsy.

"And named the kittens," said Linda with a small sob. "Soapie and Sudsie."

Billy returned and the children trailed back to Betsy's house, the express wagon rattling behind them. When they reached the house, Billy found that his little boat was dry. He picked it up and said, "Well, so long! Thanks for the paint, Betsy, and the brownies and everything."

At dinner that evening, the four girls told Betsy's father and mother all about Ralph, his cat, and the kittens. As they were eating their dessert, they heard the rattling wheels of an express wagon coming up the driveway. Betsy jumped up and looked out the

window. "It's Ralph!" she cried. "He has the box in his wagon."

"Has he got the kittens?" cried Linda.

"I don't know," said Betsy, running to the back door.

Betsy opened the back door just as Ralph reached it. "Hello, Ralph!" she said.

"Hi!" said Ralph. "My mother says I can't keep the cat and the kittens."

Ellen, Star, and Linda pressed behind Betsy so hard they almost pushed her out the door. "You mean you can't have your own cat any more?" said Ellen.

Ralph looked up. His eyes were big and round. "It's not my cat. My cat's Peter," he said.

"Father!" Betsy called. "Father! The cat and the kittens are home. Please come and get the box."

"Oh, dear!" said Ellen. "Now we shall have to unchristen Petrella."

"How do you unchristen, Ellen?" asked Linda.

"I don't know," said Ellen.

"Now we have to find out who owns her all over again," said Betsy.

"Yeah!" said Ralph. "My cat's Peter."

CHAPTER 6

HOW SOAPIE WAS DONE IN SOAP

M OTHER!" said Betsy, coming in from school one day. "Do you have a cake of Ivory soap that I can have?"

"I think there's one in the closet down beside the laundry tub," her mother replied. "What are you going to wash?"

"I'm not going to wash with it," said Betsy. "I want to carve with it. Did you ever hear of soap sculpture, Mother?"

"Yes, indeed!" replied Mother. "I've seen some beautiful pieces."

"At school we're going to have an exhibition of soap sculpture," said Betsy. "And there's going to be a prize."

"What are you planning to make?" asked Mother.

"I thought I would make a kitten," replied Betsy. "You see, I can look at Soapie and Sudsie and see how they go."

"You mean, what they look like?" asked her mother.

"Yes," replied Betsy. Then she laughed. "I'll call it Soapie in Soap. There couldn't be a better name."

Betsy took off her school dress and put on her painting smock. Then she went down to the laundry. She opened the closet door and found two cakes of soap sitting on the shelf. She took one of them and carried it to her worktable. She rummaged through a box of pencils and crayons and picked out a soft pencil and a penknife. Before she set to work she pulled her chair over by the box where the cat and the kittens were sleeping. She sat looking into the box with her chin in her hands.

Star came down the stairs. "What's the matter with the kittens?" she asked, when she saw Betsy.

"Nothing is the matter with them," said Betsy. "I'm just looking at them."

"What are they doing?" said Star.

"They're asleep," said Betsy.

"Oh! Let's wake them up and play with them," said Star.

"No!" said Betsy. "I want them to keep still so I can look at them."

Star stood beside Betsy for a few minutes while Betsy stared down at the kittens. Finally Star said, "How long are you going to look at them?"

"I have to look at them to see how they go," said Betsy.

"I don't see them going anywhere," said Star.

"I don't mean that," said Betsy. "I'm going to make a kitten."

111

"Make a kitten!" exclaimed Star. "How can you make a kitten?"

"I'm going to make one out of a cake of soap," said Betsy.

"Can I watch you?" Star asked.

"If you don't ask questions, you can," replied Betsy.

"All right," said Star.

With a soft lead pencil Betsy began to draw a cat on the side of the soap. "Oh!" said Star. "Is it going to be a flat kitten?"

"Of course not," said Betsy. "I have to draw it first, so that it will be sure to fit into the cake of soap." She turned the soap over and drew the top view of the kitten on the top of the soap.

"Why don't you make it out of yellow soap?" Star asked. "Then it would really look like Soapie."

"Because we have to make our things out of Ivory soap," said Betsy.

"Why?" asked Star.

"Because the teacher said so," replied Betsy. "And, anyway, it will look like ivory."

"Why is it good to have it look like ivory?" asked Star. "I thought you said it was to look like Soapie."

"Oh, Star! Do be quiet," said Betsy, as she began to pare little pieces of soap away with her penknife.

"All right," said Star. But in a moment she asked, "What are you going to do with the little pieces?"

"I'll put them in the washing machine for Maggie. She can use them when she does the laundry," replied Betsy.

113

Just then Betsy heard the door at the head of the stairs open. Billy's voice called out, "Hi, Betsy!" This was followed by the clatter of Billy's feet. Billy always came down the stairs as though he had been kicked off the top step. "Hi!" he said again. "What are you doing?"

"She's making a soap Soapie," said Star.

Billy looked over Betsy's shoulder. "Oh, you're doing your soap sculpture!" he said. "What's it supposed to be?"

"A kitten," said Betsy.

"Let's see it," said Billy. Betsy showed her work to Billy. "Oh, you have its head too big," said Billy. "And you'll never have room for the tail."

"Give it back," said Betsy. "The tail isn't going to stick out. It's going to curl around the kitten."

Billy handed it over. Then he said, "Anyway, I'm going to get the prize."

"How do you know?" Betsy asked.

"Because I'm artistic," said Billy. "My father is an artist. That means I have talent."

"Humph!" said Betsy. "Just wait and see."

"Well, *you* just wait and see," said Billy. "I'm going to make something different."

"Different from what?" asked Betsy.

"Different from everything," said Billy. "You just wait. I wish I had some soap. If I had, I'd start it now."

"There's another cake of soap in the closet beside the washer," said Betsy. "Star, you go ask Mother if Billy can have it."

Star went off. In a few minutes she returned. "Mother says Billy can have the soap," she said.

Billy went to the closet and took out the last cake. Soon he was adding to the pile of little chips. Betsy had no idea what Billy was making and he wouldn't tell her. Star grew tired of watching the chips of soap pile up and went off to play with her friend Lillybell.

Every once in a while Betsy took a long look at the kittens. Then she returned to her work. When Billy was ready to leave he looked at Betsy's kitten very carefully. "That doesn't look much like a kitten to me," he said.

"Well, it looks something like a kitten," said Betsy. "And your sculpture still looks like a cake of soap."

"Oh, that's what you think," said Billy, "but you don't know what I'm making."

Every day after school Betsy hurried home to work on her soap kitten. She was more and more pleased with it. Billy had taken his soap home with him, and Betsy hadn't seen it again. He was still being very mysterious about it.

At the end of the week, Betsy decided that the kitten was almost finished. She showed it to her mother, who thought it was very nice, indeed. When she showed it to Father, he said, "That's great, Betsy! It has everything except a meower."

"Do you think it will win the prize?" Betsy asked.

"I wouldn't be surprised," said Father.

"What's the prize?" asked Star.

"It's six brand-new books," said Betsy. "We can choose them from the school book list."

"I certainly hope you win them," said Father.

"Billy says he's going to win," said Betsy. "He says he has talent, because his father is an artist. He says that makes him artistic."

"Well, you tell Billy," said her father, "that your father is in the milk business, but that doesn't make you a cow."

Betsy laughed. "I'm glad of that," she said.

Betsy took her soap kitten down to the basement. She worked on the ears for a little while and decided that it was almost finished. Then she put it on the shelf inside the closet beside the laundry tub, where it wouldn't get dusty. She stood in front of it for a while, admiring it. Then she closed the door and went outside to play with Star.

The following morning the laundress, Maggie, arrived to do the laundry. She emptied the laundry hamper and carried the soiled clothes down to the basement. There she sorted them over. She set aside all of Star's and Betsy's play dresses. They always needed some special soaping to get out the dirty marks and spots. She filled the washing machine with sheets and pillowcases and towels and turned on the switch. The washer began to rumble and the water to splash. In a moment Maggie opened the door and threw some soap powder in with the wash. Then she shut the door and picked up the little girls' dresses. She put them into the laundry tub and ran some water in.

Maggie always rubbed Ivory soap on the dirty spots, so she looked around for a cake of soap. When she didn't see any, she went to the closet and opened the door. She looked on the shelf where the soap was kept, but there was no cake of soap there. She did see what she thought was a lump of soap and, without looking at it carefully, she carried it to the tub. She put one dress on the washboard and rubbed the soap on the

118

front of the skirt. "I never knew a child who got her dresses as dirty as Star," Maggie muttered to herself as she rubbed. Then she dropped the soap kitten into the tub. It floated around among the other dresses.

As she picked up each dress, Maggie plunged her hand into the warm water and picked up the soap. Then she rubbed it hard on the streaks and spots, and dropped it back into the water. Soon the soap kitten began to melt away. First its ears disappeared. Then its eyes were gone. It looked as though it had closed its eyes, never expecting to see a prize.

By the time all the spots were out of the dresses, the soap kitten had lost most of its shape. All the rest of the day it sat in the soap dish beside the laundry tub. Maggie never glanced at it again.

When Betsy came in from school, Maggie was ironing in the kitchen. "Hello, Maggie!" said Betsy.

"Hello, Betsy!" Maggie replied. "Your mother went out to do some marketing. She won't be long."

"Where is Star?" asked Betsy.

"She's over playing with Lillybell," said Maggie.

Betsy hung her coat in the closet and went downstairs. In a few minutes Maggie heard her call. "Maggie, did you see my kitten?"

Maggie opened the door. "The kittens are there. I gave them a saucer of milk just a little while ago," she called back.

"I don't mean those kittens," said Betsy. "I mean my Ivory-soap kitten."

"Honey," said Maggie, "I don't know what you're talking about." Maggie went back to her ironing. In another minute she heard Betsy scream.

Maggie opened the door again and Betsy rushed up the stairs. The remains of her soap kitten were in her hand. Tears rolled down her cheeks. "Oh, Maggie!" she cried. "My kitten is ruined! My lovely kitten! You did the washing with my kitten. Look!"

Maggie took the piece of soap in her hand and looked at it.

"I worked all week making it," Betsy sobbed. "And

it was beautiful. I was trying to win the prize at school." Betsy cried as though her heart would break.

"Oh, honey!" said Maggie. "I never looked at it. I picked it up, because it was the only piece of soap in the closet. My goodness! What can I do?" Now big tears stood in Maggie's eyes. "You know I wouldn't have done that to you for anything in the world, honey," she said. She sat down on the kitchen chair and held her head. The tears ran down her cheeks.

Betsy was surprised to see Maggie cry. "Oh, Maggie," she sobbed, "what shall we do?"

Maggie reached out and put her arm around Betsy and Betsy put her head on Maggie's shoulder. Suddenly the door opened and Star came into the kitchen. She looked at Betsy and Maggie clinging to each other, both of them crying. "What is it? What's the matter?" said Star. Then she, too, burst into tears.

Just then Mother came in the front door with a big bag of groceries. Star rushed to her. "Mother!" she cried. "Mother!"

121

"Whatever is the matter?" asked her mother. "Star, what are you crying about?"

"I don't know," said Star. "I'm crying because Betsy and Maggie are crying."

Mother went into the kitchen. When she saw Betsy crying on Maggie's shoulder and Maggie crying into Betsy's hair, she said, "Whatever is the matter?"

"Look, Mother!" said Betsy, holding up the piece of soap. "It's ruined! Maggie didn't mean to do it, but it's ruined."

Mother put her bag of groceries on the table and sat down. She took what was once the kitten into her hands. "Now stop crying and let's see what can be done with it."

"Nothing can be done with it, Mother," said Betsy.

"Now first of all," said her mother, "let's try to forget it was a kitten and see what it looks like now." She turned the piece of soap around and around. "Maybe you can make something out of it that will be even better than the kitten."

"Oh, Mother!" cried Betsy. "It's ruined."

"Betsy," said her mother, "if you don't look, you won't see."

Betsy was interested now. She leaned over her mother and looked at the soap. Finally she sniffed and said, "It looks a little bit like a mouse."

"Why, it does, Betsy!" said her mother. "I believe if you work on it, you can turn it into a lovely little white mouse."

"But I haven't any mouse to look at," said Betsy.

Star, who had been listening, dashed up to her bedroom. When she returned, she said, "Here, Betsy! Here is a book with pictures of a mouse."

Betsy took the book down to the winterhouse. As she went out the door, she said to Maggie, "It's going to be a mouse now, Maggie."

"Oh, I'm so glad!" said Maggie. "It will be a great surprise to the kitten to be turned into a mouse, I'd say."

Betsy worked on her piece of soap until it really

125

looked like a little white mouse. When the day arrived for Betsy to take it to school, she was very proud of it. She knew that it was even better than the kitten had been. When she returned from school, Maggie was ironing in the kitchen again. "Oh, Maggie!" cried Betsy. "I won the prize. My white mouse won the prize."

"That's wonderful news," said Maggie. "It certainly makes me feel better."

"Billy said he was going to get the prize," said Star, who was standing by the kitchen table, eating bread and jelly.

"Oh, Billy's just looked like a round cake of soap. Nobody knew what it was, but he said it was a flying saucer."

"Was it a good flying saucer?" asked Star.

"Maybe it was and maybe it wasn't," said Betsy. "Nobody could tell, because nobody had ever seen one."

"Well, it was different," said Billy, who had just burst into the kitchen through the back door. "I came over to help you make out your list of books for the prize, Betsy. You will let me read them, won't you?"

"Don't think you're going to get the prize that way," said Betsy. But Billy just laughed. He knew his friend Betsy.

CHAPTER 7

LOST-AND-FOUND CATS

THE washing-machine kittens were growing and they were getting very frisky. Betsy had inquired all around the neighborhood, but she could not find the owner of the mother cat. So the cat went on living with her kittens at Betsy's house.

Since the cat had been christened Petrella, all the children tried to call her Petrella. But it was hard to

say, "Here, Petrella! Petrella! Petrella!" So very soon
they shortened her name to Elly. Everyone had ac-
cepted Elly, even Thumpy, but Betsy's mother felt
that the kittens should be given away. Betsy and Star
were sorry to let them go, but they agreed with Mother
that three cats were too many cats for their house.

One afternoon, when Betsy was walking home from
school, she met Ralph. "Hello, Ralph!" she called to
him.

"Hi!" said Ralph.

"Did you ever find your cat that you lost?" asked
Betsy.

"No," said Ralph. "I guess he's lost for keeps. Do
you still have those nice kittens?"

"Oh, yes!" replied Betsy. "And we still have the
mother cat, too. We never found out who owned her."

"I wish I could have one of those kittens," said
Ralph.

"Would your mother let you have one?" asked Betsy.

"Maybe," said Ralph. "I can ask her."

"I'll wait here," said Betsy. "You go ask her."

"O.K.!" said Ralph, and he dashed into the house. In a few minutes he came out again. His face was shining. "I can have one!" he shouted, as he ran toward Betsy. "Mommy says I can have one."

"Well, come along home with me," said Betsy. "You can pick the one you want."

"I know which one I want," said Ralph. "I want the Sudsie one."

"You'll take good care of it, won't you?" Betsy asked. "You won't let it get lost, will you?"

"Oh, no!" said Ralph. "I didn't let Peter get lost. He just lost himself."

When Betsy and Ralph reached Betsy's house, they went downstairs to see the kittens. Soon Star joined them. "What are you doing?" Star asked.

"Ralphie is going to take Sudsie," said Betsy.

Star sighed. "Oh, dear!" she said. "Elly and Soapie will miss Sudsie."

"Oh, I'll bring Sudsie over to see them," said **Ralph.** "She can come over to play with Soapie."

"Sudsie is a he," said Betsy. "Soapie is a she."

"All right," said Ralph. "I'll bring him over to see his mother and his sister."

"Well, don't forget," said Star.

Ralph gathered Sudsie up in his arms and carried him upstairs. "He's a nice kitten," said Ralph.

Later in the afternoon Ellen and Linda came to play with Betsy and Star. When Linda discovered that one of the kittens was gone, she cried out, "Oh! Where's Sudsie?"

"We gave Sudsie to Ralph, because he never found his cat Peter," said Betsy.

"Are you going to give Soapie to me?" Linda asked.

"Linda!" said Ellen. "You know Mother said you could not have another cat. You have Tobey and Mother says one cat is enough."

"But Soapie isn't a cat, Ellen," said Linda. "Soapie is a kitten."

133

"But Soapie will grow up to be a cat," Ellen replied. "And then we would have two cats."

Linda turned to Betsy and said, "What are you going to do with Soapie?"

"We'll find someone who will love her and give her a good home," replied Betsy.

Linda began to cry. "I love her already," she said. "I would give her a good home."

"Linda!" said Ellen. "Stop crying. You can't have the kitten."

When it was time for Ellen and Linda to go home, Linda said, "You won't give Soapie to anyone today, will you, Betsy?"

"Not today," replied Betsy.

"And not tomorrow?" asked Linda.

"I don't know about tomorrow," said Betsy.

Linda began to cry again. "Promise me, not tomorrow," she cried.

"All right," said Betsy. "I promise."

That night Linda lay awake in her bed, thinking.

If she didn't have Tobey, she thought, she could have Soapie. But she loved Tobey! She loved Tobey very much. But she did want Soapie. Soapie was such a cute kitten. She thought of Ralph, who had lost his cat and now had Sudsie.

Linda's thoughts returned to Tobey. If Tobey was lost, she could have Soapie. Suddenly she had an idea. She would hide Tobey and everyone would think that Tobey was lost. Then she could have Soapie. With this happy idea Linda fell asleep.

The next morning, after Ellen had left for school, Linda gathered Tobey into her arms and set out to find a place to hide him. She walked for two blocks, thinking up a long story. It was all about cat catchers. Tobey was getting very heavy. Linda shifted him. She was afraid to put him down, because he might run away.

When Linda reached the middle of the next block, she saw a red police car coming toward her. It was Mr. Kilpatrick, the policeman. She knew Mr. Kilpatrick very well. She saw him every afternoon when she went to kindergarten, for he took her across the wide street near school.

When Mr. Kilpatrick reached Linda, he stopped his car. "Where are you going with the cat?" he called to Linda.

"I'm going over to Betsy's house," said Linda. "Tobey's awful heavy."

"Well, climb in beside me," said Mr. Kilpatrick. "I'll run you around to Betsy's house."

Mr. Kilpatrick opened the door of his car, and Linda put Tobey on the seat beside Mr. Kilpatrick. Then she climbed in. She settled herself beside Mr. Kilpatrick and took Tobey on her lap.

"Are you taking your cat to see little Star?" Mr. Kilpatrick asked.

"I have to hide Tobey," Linda said in a whisper.

"You don't say!" said Mr. Kilpatrick. "Why do you have to hide Tobey?"

"The cat catchers are after him," said Linda.

"Cat catchers!" said Mr. Kilpatrick. "I don't believe I know about the cat catchers."

"You know what dogcatchers are, don't you?" asked Linda.

"Oh, sure!" said Mr. Kilpatrick.

"Well, the cat catchers catch cats, just like the dogcatchers catch dogs," said Linda.

"Oh!" said Mr. Kilpatrick.

A few minutes later Mr. Kilpatrick stopped in front of Betsy's house and Linda stepped out of the red car. She picked up Tobey and said, "Thank you for bringing me."

"You're quite welcome," said Mr. Kilpatrick. "Don't be late for kindergarten this afternoon."

"I won't," said Linda.

"And don't forget where you hide your cat," said Mr. Kilpatrick.

"I won't," said Linda.

Star came out of the house just as Linda pushed open the front gate. "Hello, Linda!" Star called out. "What are you doing with Tobey?"

"I have to hide him," said Linda, looking very mysterious.

"Why?" asked Star.

"The cat catchers are after him," said Linda.

"Oh!" said Star. "They are?"

"Yes, they are," said Linda. "Poor Tobey! I don't know where to hide him."

Star looked all around. Then she looked up in the tree.

"We can't put Tobey in a tree," said Linda.

Star looked back at the Jacksons' house, where Lillybell lived. Linda looked too. She saw the bathhouse near the Jacksons' swimming pool. "Star!" said Linda. "Maybe we could hide Tobey in the bathhouse over at Mr. Jackson's."

"Maybe," said Star.

The two little girls walked through the garden behind Star's house to the stone wall that separated her garden from the Jacksons' garden. "You climb over first, Star," said Linda. "Then you can hold Tobey while I climb over."

Star climbed over the wall. She held out her arms for Tobey and Linda handed him over. Then Linda climbed over the wall.

The children walked past the empty swimming pool and over to the bathhouse. Star turned the knob on one of the doors and pushed. The door opened. "Just open it a little bit," said Linda.

Star opened it a little bit and Linda pushed Tobey through the opening. Then Star quickly pulled the door shut. "He will starve," said Star.

"Oh!" cried Linda. "Oh! You'll have to feed him. But you mustn't tell anyone where Tobey is."

"Why?" asked Star.

"Because they might tell the cat catchers," said Linda.

"Oh! All right!" said Star. "But I don't think Betsy would tell the cat catchers."

"You mustn't tell Betsy!" Linda cried.

"All right," said Star. "I won't tell her."

"Well, good-by!" said Linda. "I have to go home now."

"Good-by!" said Star.

Linda went off and Star climbed over the stone wall, back into her own garden.

Late in the afternoon Star poured some milk into a dish and carried it outside. She carried it carefully as far as the garden wall. There she placed it on the wall while she climbed over. She picked it up and went on to the bathhouse. She opened the door very carefully, and called, "Here, Tobey!"

Tobey said, "Meow!" when he saw that Star had a dish of milk.

Star set the dish down on the floor, and Tobey began to lap up the milk. Then she went out, closing the door carefully.

That evening Linda's mother said to her, "I haven't seen Tobey all day."

"Poor Tobey!" said Linda. "I guess he's lost."

"I hope not," said her mother. "You would miss Tobey. You love Tobey so much."

"I guess he's lost," said Linda. "Ralph lost his cat and it never came back. I guess I'll have to get a new cat."

"Oh, he'll come back," said her mother.

"I don't think so," said Linda. "I guess I better go over to Betsy's and get Soapie."

"Why, Linda!" said her mother. "I am surprised at you. Don't you want Tobey back?"

"Poor Tobey!" said Linda. "He was a nice cat. May I have the kitten, Mommie?"

"We'll wait and see if Tobey comes back," said her mother.

"Couldn't I have the kitten until he comes back?" Linda begged.

"Wait and see," said her mother.

That night, as Mr. Jackson was going upstairs to bed, he heard a cat crying. He went outside and looked around. The cry came from down by the swimming pool. Mr. Jackson thought that perhaps a cat had fallen into the empty pool and couldn't get out. He walked along the path that led past the bathhouse. When he reached the bathhouse he knew that the cat was inside. He opened the door and the cat ran out and disappeared in the darkness.

The following morning Linda went over to the Jacksons' bathhouse to visit Tobey. She opened the door and said, "Hello, Tobey!" There was no sound. She looked around on the floor but there was no Tobey. She got down on her hands and knees and looked under a bench. She called, "Here, Tobey! Here, Tobey!"

The bathhouse was empty. Tobey was gone. Linda went outside and called, "Tobey!" Tobey didn't come. She called again, "Tobey!" There was no sign of Tobey.

Linda ran as fast as her legs could carry her. She ran all the way home. She burst into the house, crying, "Mommie! Mommie!"

"What's the matter, Linda?" her mother called from upstairs.

Linda climbed the stairs, screaming, "Mommie! Tobey is gone! Tobey is gone! He's lost, Mommie! He's lost!" Linda threw her arms around her mother's knees and hid her face against her mother's apron. "Oh, Mommie!" she sobbed. "I've lost Tobey."

Linda's mother patted her head and said, "Why, Linda! You didn't seem to feel bad last night, when you said Tobey was lost."

"But he's really lost now," Linda sobbed. "I'll never see Tobey again. I went over to Mr. Jackson's and Tobey was gone."

"What has Mr. Jackson to do with it?" her mother asked.

Linda sobbed a few minutes. Then she said, "I hid Tobey in Mr. Jackson's bathhouse. I hid him so that you would let me have the kitten." She began to cry again.

"That was a very naughty thing to do, Linda," said her mother. "Now if Tobey is lost, it is your own fault."

"I know," sobbed Linda. "I would rather have Tobey than any kitten in the world. He's my own Tobey and I want him back."

"Well, we shall just have to hope that he will find his way home," said her mother.

Tobey had not returned by the time Linda came home from kindergarten. Ellen telephoned Betsy to find out if they had seen anything of Tobey. No one had seen him. A very sad little Linda went to bed without Tobey. She cried some more and finally fell asleep.

About ten o'clock Linda's mother put the milk bottles out by the back door for the milkman. There was Tobey, his eyes shining in the darkness. "Oh, Tobey!" said Linda's mother. "Where have you been?" She opened the back door and Tobey ran into the kitchen.

146

Linda's mother opened a can of cat food and gave Tobey a saucerful. He ate it all up. Then she picked him up and carried him upstairs to Linda's room. Tobey jumped up on the foot of Linda's bed, where he always slept. Soon he was settled for the night.

The next morning, when Linda woke up, she felt something moving on the foot of her bed. She sat up and there was Tobey, stepping over the bedcovers and coming toward her. Linda took him in her arms and buried her face in his fur. "Oh, Tobey!" she said. "I'm so glad you came back."

Then she called out at the top of her voice, "Ellen! Ellen! Tobey is back."

Ellen came in to see Tobey. "I'm so glad he's back," she said.

"Ellen," said Linda, "you tell Betsy that I don't want Soapie. She can give Soapie to somebody else, because I have my Tobey. He's the nicest cat in the whole world."

CHAPTER 8

APRIL FOOL FOR WHOM?

BETSY and Ellen and Billy had been working on a puppet show in Betsy's winterhouse. They had spent weeks getting everything together for their first performance.

Ellen had written most of the play with suggestions from Betsy and Billy. They had built the stage out of a strong packing box. It had a red velvet curtain, which Betsy had made out of a piece of one of Mother's old dresses. The children had decided to name the puppet theater the Winterhouse Puppet Theater. On each side of the curtain there was a large gold *W,* which Ellen had cut out of the lid of a candy box. The girls thought the letters made the curtain very beautiful. The puppets were made out of clothespins, and Betsy and Ellen spent hours making their clothes.

There had been a great deal of arguing before the children decided about the play. There was more argument while the play was being written. Billy wanted a mystery play. "A real thriller," he had said. Ellen, of course, wanted it to be a fairy-tale play. Betsy had a piece of plaid material left from one of her dresses, which she wanted to make into kilts.

Ellen said, "Oh, well! It can still be a fairy-tale play and we can have it in Scotland and somebody can wear kilts."

"Sure!" said Billy. "The fairies can wear kilts."

"Oh, Billy! Don't be silly!" said Ellen. "Whoever heard of fairies wearing kilts!"

"Aw, Ellen! You always want fairies!" said Billy. "Why don't you grow up? Let's have a real thriller with a ghost in it."

"Billy," said Ellen. "You wanted to make the scenery and I was to write the play, so I think I should have fairies if I want fairies."

Billy looked at Betsy and shook his head. "I believe Ellen thinks there really are fairies," he said. "She believes in fairies."

"Well, ghosts aren't real either, and I think it's much nicer to believe in fairies," said Betsy, "than to believe in ghosts."

Billy, for the moment, was left without words. Before he could think of anything to say, Betsy added, "It's just the same, Billy. Ellen makes believe there are little fairies and you make believe there are big ghosts." Then she turned to Ellen and said, "Go ahead, Ellen, and write the play. And don't forget, it has to be in Scotland, because I want to use this plaid material."

So Ellen began to write a play about a princess who lived in a castle in the highlands of Scotland. She lived

with a wicked uncle. "He can wear the kilts," said Ellen.

"Oh, no!" said Betsy. "I don't want him to wear the kilts. I want somebody who's nice to wear the kilts. Isn't there a prince?"

"Oh, yes," said Ellen. "The prince! I think he should play a violin or something."

"Bagpipes!" Betsy cried. "They play bagpipes in Scotland."

"All right," said Ellen. "He comes and plays a bagpipe and sings to the princess." Then, turning to Billy, she said, "Billy, when you build the castle, be sure to make it with a balcony. The prince will stand under the balcony and play his bagpipes and sing."

"How can he play a bagpipe and sing at the same time?" asked Billy. "He has to blow the bagpipe. He can't blow and sing at the same time."

"Oh!" said Ellen. "I guess he better just play the bagpipe then."

"He better just sing," said Billy. "If he plays a bagpipe, that princess's wicked uncle is going to come out on that balcony and throw a bucket of water on that prince."

"Have him sing," said Betsy. "He can sing *Annie Laurie*. That's a Scotch song and we can play it on the record player. A bagpipe would be awfully hard to make, anyway." Betsy tore off a piece of plaid material and began pleating it into a kilt. "Go on with the story of the play, Ellen."

"Oh, I forgot to tell you," said Ellen, "the prince comes in a flying saucer."

"Yippee!" cried Billy. "Now you're getting somewhere."

"Oh, Ellen!" said Betsy. "The prince can't wear kilts and come in a flying saucer! If he comes in a flying saucer, he's a space man, and space men don't wear kilts."

"Oh, make him a space man," said Billy. "Put the kilts back on the wicked uncle."

"No. Billy," said Betsy, "you are making a mess of this play."

"I know how to fix it!" said Billy. "Is this prince guy finally going to marry the princess?"

"Of course!" said Ellen.

"Well then, they can go off in the flying saucer. People always go off in something when they get married."

"O.K.," said Ellen.

"Where do the fairies come in?" asked Betsy.

"There is a good fairy, of course," said Ellen. "She will wear white. She always follows the princess wherever she goes. Then there is a bad fairy. She will be dressed all in black. She follows the wicked uncle everywhere."

"I don't think this play is any good," said Billy. "It sounds just like any old play. The princess, the prince, somebody wicked, a good fairy, a bad fairy. This play needs something exciting in it."

"What?" said Ellen.

"I'll tell you," said Billy. "This castle in Scotland is haunted. There's a skeleton that walks through the halls in the dead of night, dragging a heavy chain. I can rattle something and make it sound like a chain. That would really be good. It's so dark down here when the lights are out that everybody will be scared right off their seats."

"No, Billy!" said Betsy. "We are not going to have a scary play. When Star and Linda get frightened they cry, and Linda always cries so loud she has to be taken out of the room, because nobody is able to hear anything."

"Oh! You and Ellen would get scared, too," said Billy. "You're both scared of the dark."

"We are not!" the two girls called out in a chorus.

"You're scared of your shadow," said Billy.

"We are not!" shouted Betsy and Ellen.

"Tell you what!" said Ellen. "Some place in the play you can rattle the chains and the princess can say, 'Forsooth, yon sound is the castle's ghost!'"

"What does *forsooth* mean?" asked Billy.

"They always say *forsooth*," said Ellen.

"Well, forsooth, let's have the door swing open and show a skeleton," said Billy.

"No!" said Betsy. "Anyway, it's too hard to make a clothespin into a skeleton."

"You're just scared!" said Billy.

"I am not," said Betsy. "I just don't think it's necessary to have a skeleton."

The play was finally written to the satisfaction of Betsy and Ellen. Then they chose the records to play on the record player. They chose so many that the play turned into a musical. Billy said it sure needed something. If it couldn't have a skeleton, it had better have music. This, of course, meant more characters, because, as Betsy pointed out, musicals have choruses and ballets. They had to go out and buy more clothespins. Betsy put the whole ballet in kilts.

Although Billy thought little of the production, he was interested in building the scenery. He also liked to see what he could do with the lights. The flying saucer that he made out of cardboard was much better than the one he had made out of Ivory soap.

Finally Betsy and Ellen and Billy announced to their friends that the first production of the Winterhouse Puppet Theater would be given on April 1. Billy printed the tickets with a printing stamp that he had.

156

He read over the first one. It said: The Winterhouse Puppet Theater presents *The Golden Princess,* Saturday evening, April 1 at 7:30 P.M. When he looked at April 1, Billy suddenly thought, April Fools' Day!

Billy loved ᴬApril Fools' Day, because he loved to play tricks on his friends. He began to think up a few tricks. First of all, he decided to change the name of the musical. He held his printing stamp in his hand and picked out the letters that spelled *The Golden Princess* and put in *The Castle Ghost.* Then he printed the tickets.

The following day Billy took the tickets to school and gave some of them to Betsy and some to Ellen. Neither Betsy nor Ellen read them. They were too anxious to begin selling their tickets for five cents apiece. By the end of the day Betsy had sold two tickets—one to Mr. Jackson and one to Mrs. Jackson. Ellen had sold one to her mother. Billy had done better. He had sold one to Mary Lou and two to Mr. Kilpatrick, who promised to bring his wife.

The next day Mary Lou brought her ticket back. She took it to Betsy and said, "Look, Betsy! I want my five cents back. I don't like ghost stories."

"But it isn't a ghost story," said Betsy.

"It says right here on the ticket, *The Castle Ghost,*" said Mary Lou.

Betsy looked at the ticket. Her eyes grew very round as she read it. "Why—why!" she exclaimed. "Why, that isn't the name at all. It's called *The Golden Princess.*"

The bell rang for school to begin before Betsy could speak to Billy. Once she caught his eye and pointed to the ticket. Then she made a face like a thundercloud. At recess time she pounced on him. "Billy Porter!" she said. "You deliberately changed the name of our musical. No wonder we can't sell the tickets! I have to give Mary Lou her nickel back."

"Oh, it was just an April Fool joke," said Billy.

"You keep your jokes until April Fool," said Betsy,

"and don't try any around our house. Now you will have to print those tickets over."

Billy printed them over, but while he was doing it he thought of another April Fool joke. This one, he decided, would keep until the night of the performance.

The new tickets didn't sell any better than the first ones, so finally Betsy called a meeting of the directors of the Winterhouse Puppet Theater. The directors, of course, were Billy, Ellen, and herself. Betsy said the tickets were hard to sell.

Ellen said, "Yes, they are."

Billy said, "There's no use giving a show if there isn't a crowd to see it."

So the directors voted to give the tickets away and to return the money to Mr. Kilpatrick, Mr. and Mrs. Jackson, and Ellen's mother. This was hard to do and it would take a little time, because they had already spent the twenty-five cents for gumdrops.

The following day, when they announced to their friends that the tickets for the puppet show were free, everyone wanted one. They all wanted one for themselves and one for their fathers and one for their mothers. Soon all the tickets were gone.

Billy could hardly wait for the night of the performance to come. He kept thinking about the April Fool joke he was planning. He had decided to dress up in the costume he had worn on Halloween. It was a skin-tight black suit with a white skeleton painted on it in paint that glowed in the dark. He planned to let himself into the basement of Betsy's house through the cellar window. He would go in while Betsy and Star and their father and mother were having their dinner. Then he would slip into the winterhouse and hide under the table where the puppet show was set up. The table had a black cover that hung down to the floor. He would sit under the table until everyone arrived. Then, when all the lights went out and the place was as dark as night, he would rattle his chains. Then

162

he would crawl out, rise up behind the puppet theater, wave his arms around, and scare everyone stiff.
Betsy and Ellen would see that their show really was
haunted.

On the afternoon of April Fools' Day Billy came
over to Betsy's to see if everything was set for the
performance. While Betsy and Ellen were busy putting the final touches on the puppets, Billy went into
the laundry. He climbed up on top of the washing
machine and unlocked the window above the washer.

When he came back into the winterhouse, Betsy and
Ellen were rehearsing with the puppets. "Oh, I do
hope everything goes all right," said Betsy.

"I hope the prince doesn't lose his kilt," said Billy.

"He won't," said Betsy. "It's fastened on with two
thumbtacks."

Billy tried the lights; then he said, "I guess I'll get
along."

"Don't be late tonight," Ellen called after him.

"Oh, no!" said Billy. "You can count on me."

Billy went home and bolted his dinner. When he asked to be excused from the table, he said, "I have to get over to Betsy's early, 'cause of the show." He went upstairs and put on his Halloween costume. He put on everything except the head. Then he put his raincoat on and stuck the head in his pocket.

When he came downstairs, his father said, "Why the raincoat?"

"It might rain," said Billy. "Looks a little cloudy."

"That's the first time you ever thought of that," said his mother. "Usually you're soaked through to your skin before you notice that it's raining."

Billy paid no attention to this remark. Instead he said, "Are you and Dad coming to the show?"

"We'll be over," his mother replied.

Billy went to Betsy's on his bicycle. When he arrived, he wheeled his bicycle up to the garage. It was open so he placed it inside. He took the head of his costume out of his pocket and put his raincoat in the basket on his bicycle. Then he put his head on and tiptoed around the house to the cellar window that he had unlocked. As he passed the dining-room windows he could see Betsy's father's head at the dinner table. He knew that the coast was clear.

It was easy to crawl through the cellar window. He let down his feet until they touched the top of the washing machine. Then he dropped to the floor. The whole basement was pitch dark. Billy looked ahead of him. In the blackness beyond stood a white skele-

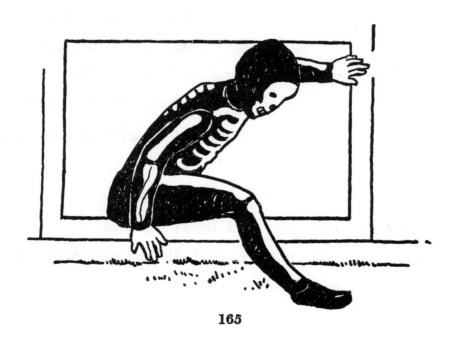

ton. It seemed to Billy to fill the whole basement. He opened his mouth and let out a piercing scream. He ran screaming and stumbling in the darkness until he reached the cellar stairs.

As he rushed up the stairs, Betsy's father opened the cellar door. Billy fell over his own feet and went sprawling into the kitchen. Betsy and Star and their mother stood speechless. They looked down at Billy on the floor, and Star cried, "What is it? What is it?"

"It's somebody in a Halloween suit," said Betsy.

"There's a skeleton in the basement!" Billy gasped.

Betsy recognized Billy's voice. "Why, it's Billy!" she said. "Billy, what are you doing dressed up like that?"

Betsy's father had snapped on the lights in the basement. He went down the stairs.

"Is it still there?" Billy called down.

"Come down here," said Betsy's father.

Billy went downstairs, and Betsy and Star and Mother followed.

"Where was the skeleton you saw?" asked Betsy's father.

"It was right over there," said Billy. Billy pointed to the wall and, as he looked, he saw himself reflected in a big piece of an old mirror.

"You just saw yourself, Billy," said Father.

"Oh!" said Billy. "When I saw that thing I forgot what I had on. And it looked so big, much bigger than me."

"What are you doing in that suit, anyway?" asked Betsy. "It isn't Halloween, you know."

"I know," said Billy, "but it's April Fool, and I thought I would fool everybody."

Betsy and Star and their father and mother laughed very hard. "Well, you certainly fooled yourself," said Father.

"I don't know how I forgot what I had on," said Billy. "Now I guess I better go home and put on my right clothes."

"Hurry up," said Betsy. "You know you have to work the lights for this first performance of *The Golden Princess.*"

"You bet!" said Billy. "I'm glad it isn't *The Castle Ghost.* I've had enough for tonight. Boy! Did I scare myself!"

CHAPTER 9

MAY BASKETS

Now, with each passing day, the sun grew warmer. The willow trees were already yellow-green, and the budding leaves on the maple trees were red. The tulips were pushing up in the gardens and the crocuses were in bloom. Spring had come. Betsy and Star played out of doors more than they did in the winter-house.

"Father," said Betsy one evening, "isn't it time to open up the summerhouse?"

"I'll take the boards off it about the first of May," said Father.

"There should be a celebration," said Betsy.

"Betsy!" said her father. "I never knew anyone who could think of so many reasons for celebrations."

"We should have a May Day celebration," said Betsy. "With a May queen."

Star piped up and said, "You have cellar-brations in the winterhouse, Betsy, not in the summerhouse." Everyone laughed. Star laughed too, but she didn't know what she was laughing at.

The last week in April Betsy decided to make May baskets. She had earned some money minding Mrs. Jackson's baby, so she went to the five-and-ten-cent store and bought nine little baskets. Then she bought some pink ribbon.

Betsy spent the rest of the week weaving the pink ribbon around the edge of each basket. She tied a bow on the top of each handle and added another ribbon that ended in a loop. She would use the loop to hang the basket. Betsy made her May baskets in her bedroom instead of downstairs in the winterhouse, because she wanted to keep them a secret. No one could hide a secret in the winterhouse, because Betsy's friends treated the winterhouse as though it were their own.

When Star saw the baskets, she said, "Are they Easter baskets, Betsy?"

"No," replied Betsy. "These are May baskets."

"What are May baskets?" Star asked.

"They are little baskets of flowers," said Betsy. "You hang them on people's doors on May Day."

"When is May Day?" asked Star.

"It's next Friday," said Betsy. "The first of May. I haven't very much time."

"Where are you going to hang them?" Star asked.

"I'm going to hang one on Mrs. Jackson's front door and one on the kitchen door for Lillybell's mother, because she cooks in the kitchen. Then I have one to hang on Mrs. Kilpatrick's door and one on Ellen's and one on Billy Porter's."

"Oh!" said Star.

Betsy continued, "Then I have one for Mrs. Robbins across the street and one for each of the houses next door and one for Mother."

Betsy planned to gather flowers for her baskets after school on Thursday. She wondered how she would be able to keep her friends from coming along. They were bound to say, "Where are you going?" or, "What are you going to do?" If she said, "I'm going to pick flowers," they would all say, "I'll go with you." She need not have worried. On Thursday it rained all day. After school everyone hurried to climb into the buses. No one wanted to walk home.

It was no day to pick flowers, but Betsy started out with her raincoat and rubbers and umbrella. She knew a place, not too far from school, where violets grew. They grew in thick clumps, and Betsy had gathered

great big bunches of them the year before in the spring. She had brought a large brown paper bag with her. She would put the violets into the bag. When she reached home, she planned to put the violets in water and to fix her baskets early in the morning.

Betsy had told Mother about the May baskets, because Mother would have to drive her around the neighborhood to deliver them. They would have to get up very early in order to hang them before school.

The ground was wet and soggy when she reached the place where the violets grew. Betsy was glad she was wearing her rubbers. She looked all around for the blue of the violets, but the field was full of nothing but the green leaves of the little plants. There were some buds but there were no flowers.

Betsy's heart sank. How could she fill the May baskets if she had no flowers? She stood under her umbrella for a time, feeling very unhappy. The rain seemed wetter than before and it had grown colder. Betsy shivered. There was nothing to do but go home.

175

so she sloshed through the puddles in the field and took a short cut to her home.

Betsy felt better when she reached home. A fire burned in the living room. Star and Thumpy were both lying on the rug in front of the fireplace. She found her mother in the kitchen. "Oh, Mother!" she burst out. "There are no violets at all. Whatever shall I do about the May baskets?"

"Dear child," said her mother, "you look so soggy."

"I feel soggy," said Betsy. "I worked so hard to make those May baskets."

"I know you did, darling," her mother replied. "Take off your things and set the table for me. After dinner we'll find some way to take care of the May baskets."

"I don't know how we can take care of the May baskets without flowers," said Betsy.

"Well, all you need to know right now is how to set the table," said Mother.

Betsy hung up her raincoat and got out the silver.

176

She set the table and helped her mother in the kitchen. It was a pretty kitchen, all blue and white. There was a long window with a wide window sill. Here Mother kept her begonia plants. They were in full bloom and covered with waxy, cherry-red flowers. They made the kitchen very gay.

After dinner Betsy went up to her room. She looked at her nine empty May baskets, sitting on her window sill. Whatever can I do with them, she wondered. She sat down in her chair by the lamp and opened her geography book. She did her lesson for the next day. Then she did her arithmetic and went over her spelling.

Just as Betsy finished, her mother came upstairs. "Betsy," said her mother, coming into her room, "I have an idea!"

"What is it?" Betsy asked.

"Let's take the baskets downstairs," said Mother. "I'll show you."

Betsy and her mother carried the baskets downstairs

to the kitchen and put them on the table. Mother put a little glass custard cup in one of the baskets. She poured a little bit of water into the cup. Then she stuffed some green tissue paper around the cup to hold it steady.

Betsy watched her mother with great interest. She saw her pick up the scissors, and, to her surprise, Mother began snipping little sprigs of flowers off her begonia plants. Then she stuck them into the cup in the May basket. With each new little sprig of red blossoms and shiny green leaves, the basket grew more beautiful. "Oh, Mother!" exclaimed Betsy. "That's beautiful! But you'll spoil your plants if you cut enough to fill all the baskets."

"More blossoms will come out," said her mother. "They won't look bad very long. Come, fix your baskets. I'll cut the flowers."

Betsy set to work. She put a custard cup into each basket and poured a little water into each cup. Then she stuffed in green paper as she had seen Mother do.

178

Meanwhile, the begonia blossoms piled up on the table beside the baskets.

When all the baskets were filled, Betsy thought they were the prettiest May baskets she had ever seen. She thought they were much gayer than they would have been filled with violets. "Aren't they beautiful?" said Betsy. Then she turned to her mother and threw her arms around her. "Oh, Mother!" she said. "You're so good to me. You spoiled your lovely plants just for my May baskets."

"The plants will grow again," said her mother, patting Betsy. "After all, one of these May baskets is for me."

Betsy laughed and said, "You can pick out the one you like best."

Mother picked out her May basket and set it aside. "That will look lovely hanging on the door knocker tomorrow," she said.

Betsy went to bed feeling very happy.

The following morning Mother called her early.

"Come, Betsy!" she said. "We have to hang your **May** baskets this morning."

Betsy jumped out of her bed and ran to the window. The rain was over and the pavements were dry. It was going to be a nice day.

After their early breakfast, Mother and Betsy set out in the car with the baskets. They left Father having breakfast with Star. While Mother placed the baskets on the floor of the car, Betsy carried one across the street and hung it on Mrs. Robbins' door knocker. Then she took one to each house next to her own and hung them on their knockers. When she had finished delivering these three baskets, she climbed into the car beside Mother. "The flowers look so fresh," she said.

The first stop was around the block at the Jacksons'. Betsy picked up two baskets. She climbed the porch steps and walked across the porch to the front door. In a moment she had one basket fastened to the knocker. She carried the other basket around the house

to the back door. Here there was no knocker, so she had to hang it on the doorknob.

Betsy tried to do it very quietly, because she knew that Lillybell's mother was preparing breakfast in the kitchen. The odor of coffee brewing and bacon frying was coming out through the ventilator. She heard the bang of the oven door.

But Lillybell's mother had sharp ears. She heard someone at the back door, so she pulled it open. There, to her surprise, was Betsy with a basket of flowers in her hand and her mouth wide open.

Lillybell's mother opened her mouth wide, too. "Land sakes!" she said. "What are you doing out with a basket of flowers so early in the morning?"

"Oh, dear!" said Betsy. "It was to be a surprise. It's a May basket."

"Now, isn't that lovely!" said Lillybell's mother. "I'll close the door and make believe I never opened it. You hang your basket and I'll let Lillybell find it. That's mighty sweet, Betsy. A May basket! I never had one before. Lillybell will be so excited!"

"There's one on the front door for Mr. and Mrs. Jackson," Betsy whispered.

Lillybell's mother threw her hands up and said, "They will be delighted. I won't say a word. I'll let them find it."

"Good-by!" said Betsy. "I have to go now."

"Good-by, honey!" said Lillybell's mother.

Betsy hung the basket on the doorknob. She knew that Lillybell would love to find it there. Back in the car she told her mother about being caught at the back door.

The next stop was at Ellen's house. It only took Betsy a moment to jump out of the car and hang a basket on the doorknob. When she returned to the car, she said, "Now I guess the Porters are next."

Betsy's mother laughed. "Do you think you can put that basket on the Porters' door without Billy catching you at it?"

"I don't know," said Betsy with a chuckle. "Billy is pretty sharp."

As the car stopped in front of the Porters' house, Mother accidentally leaned on the horn. It let out a blast. "Oh, Mother!" exclaimed Betsy.

"I'm sorry," said Mother.

The words were hardly out of her mouth, when the front door flew open and Billy rushed out. "Hi, Betsy!" he cried. "What are you doing? What have you got there?"

"Oh, Billy!" said Betsy. "It was to be a surprise."

"What's it for?" said Billy, looking at the basket of flowers in Betsy's hand.

"It's a May basket," said Betsy.

"What do you do with it?" Billy interrupted.

"You hang it on the front door," said Betsy. "I was going to surprise your mother."

"Well, she'll be surprised," said Billy. "Sure she will. I'll hang it on the door for you. Then I'll ring the bell and run around the house and go in the back door."

Now there was only one basket left, the one for the Kilpatricks. "I do hope Mr. and Mrs. Kilpatrick don't catch me," said Betsy. "I guess they get up early, because Mr. Kilpatrick always has to get out early in his car."

When they reached Mr. Kilpatrick's house, Betsy opened the little white gate as quietly as she could, but Mr. Kilpatrick's sharp policeman's ears heard the latch. He looked out the upstairs window and saw Betsy tiptoeing up the front path, carrying her May basket.

Mr. Kilpatrick put his finger to his lips and motioned to his wife to come and look out the window. Mrs. Kilpatrick hurried to his side. She looked down. "Upon my soul!" said Mrs. Kilpatrick. "It's that little girl, Betsy. I do believe she's bringing us a May basket. I haven't had a May basket since I was a girl in Ireland. We used to hang them around on the first day of May."

"And, sure, that's what it is today," said Mr. Kilpatrick. They stood watching behind the curtain until Betsy went out the gate and got into the car.

"That was such fun!" said Betsy. "And they didn't see me."

"It *was* fun," said Mother. "How would you like to walk to school from here? It's early and you have plenty of time. I'd like to get home quickly."

"All right, Mother," said Betsy. "Thank you for helping me deliver the baskets." Betsy waved good-by to her mother as she turned the car around and drove off.

Betsy had walked about two blocks, when Mr. Kilpatrick stopped his red police car beside her. "Hello, Betsy!" he called to her. "Want to come along with me? You're out early this morning."

"Oh, hello, Mr. Kilpatrick!" said Betsy. "Are you on your way to school, too?"

"That I am," said Mr. Kilpatrick, as he opened the

door of his car. Betsy jumped in and Mr. Kilpatrick started off. "What do you think happened at our house this morning?" said the policeman.

"What?" asked Betsy.

"Well, first of all, do you know what a May basket is?" said Mr. Kilpatrick.

"Oh, yes!" said Betsy.

"Well, sure, this morning, when Mrs. Kilpatrick went to the front door, there was one hanging on the doorknob. Pretty as anything."

Betsy felt her cheeks grow hot. "I guess somebody put it there," she said.

"Sure, it's certain it didn't grow there," said the policeman. "Do you know who I think put it there?"

"Who?" asked Betsy.

"I think it was that Billy Porter," said Mr. Kilpatrick.

"Oh, I don't think Billy Porter would hang May baskets," said Betsy.

"You don't?" said Mr. Kilpatrick.

"No," said Betsy. "I think it was probably a girl."

"Ah! Maybe you're right," said Mr. Kilpatrick. "But who could it be?"

"What kind of flowers did it have in it, Mr. Kilpatrick?" asked Betsy.

"They were little red flowers," said Mr. Kilpatrick. "Petunias."

"Petunias!" exclaimed Betsy. "Oh, no! Not petunias! They were begonias."

"Oh! So they were begonias," said Mr. Kilpatrick. "So you have seen one of these May baskets?"

"Well, ah, there's one on Mrs. Porter's front door," said Betsy.

"Aha!" said the policeman. "Didn't I say it was Billy Porter? He put one on his mother's front door, too."

Betsy shook her head. "I don't think it was Billy Porter," she said. "I think it was a girl."

"I guess you're right," said Mr. Kilpatrick. "Do you think she wears her hair in braids tied with red ribbons?"

Betsy looked up at the big policeman and laughed. "How did you know?" she said.

Mr. Kilpatrick laughed and stopped his car in front of the school. "I'm a policeman," he said. "I like to solve mysteries."

"Was this a hard one?" Betsy asked, as she got out of the car.

"I've solved harder ones," he replied with a hearty laugh.

The following day, which was Saturday, Betsy's mother took Betsy and Star into the city to get new shoes and to have lunch at a restaurant. Betsy and Star loved to have lunch at a restaurant where they could choose what they wanted to eat.

When they reached home and turned into the driveway, Betsy looked across the yard to the summerhouse to see if her father had taken the boards off it. "Oh, Mother!" she cried. "Look at the summerhouse!"

Mother and Star both looked at the summerhouse. Red, yellow, blue, and green balloons, tied to the roof,

190

were floating over the summerhouse. Long streamers
of bright colored ribbons were blowing out from the
top of the roof. Garlands of paper flowers were looped
around the railing. "What is it for, Mother?" asked
Betsy.

Star had lost her tongue completely. She just stared
up at the balloons.

As Betsy stepped out of the car, she was suddenly
surrounded by children and grownups. They had all
run out from behind the garage. They were shouting,
"Betsy is the Queen of the May! Betsy is the Queen
of the May!"

There were all her friends from school and Linda
and Lillybell. There were Mr. and Mrs. Jackson and
Lillybell's mother. The neighbors from each side, as
well as Mrs. Robbins from across the street, were there
too. "Come! Sit on your throne, Betsy," said Ellen,
taking hold of Betsy's hand.

Ellen led Betsy to the summerhouse and everyone
followed. Inside the summerhouse, and right in the

center facing the entrance, there was a chair. It was covered with a red cloth. "Sit down," said Ellen.

Betsy sat down and Ellen picked up a wreath of flowers from under the chair. She placed it on Betsy's head. Everyone shouted, "Long live Betsy, the Queen of the May!"

"Oh!" cried Star, clapping her hands. "It's a cellar-bration." Then she sniffed the air and said, "I smell hamburgers!"